IRIS,
Messenger

IRIS,
Messenger

SARAH DEMING

Harcourt, Inc.

Orlando   Austin   New York

San Diego   Toronto   London

www.HarcourtBooks.com

Library of Congress Cataloging-in-Publication Data
Deming, Sarah.
Iris, messenger/Sarah Deming.
p.   cm.
Summary: After discovering that the immortals of Greek
mythology reside in her hometown of Middleville, Pennsylvania,
twelve-year-old Iris listens to their life stories, gaining wisdom,
beauty, and startling revelations about her past.
[1. Mythology, Greek—Fiction.   2. Pennsylvania—Fiction.]
I. Title.
PZ7.D39525Ir   2007
[Fic]—dc22   2006022943
ISBN 978-0-15-205823-4

Text set in Granjon
Designed by Lydia D'moch

DOC 7 6 5 4 3
4500276428

Printed in the United States of America

To the memory of Cara Inverson and Tony Pate,
a linden tree and an oak

IRIS,
Messenger

Chapter 1

The main difference between school and prison is that prisons release you early for good behavior. School lasts about thirteen years no matter how good you are. Also, prison has better food.

The motto of Erebus Middle School was "We ♥ Children." This gave Iris Greenwold a funny feeling in the pit of her stomach, which she would later learn was called "irony."

Iris's strategy for survival at Erebus was to be as inconspicuous as possible. The more average you seemed, the less the other kids would pick on you and the more the teachers would ignore you. This would leave you free to dream. And if there was one thing Iris Greenwold was good at, it was dreaming. She was always making up stories about imaginary people. Iris preferred imaginary people. They were more interesting than real ones. Whenever she had to write a report, she would try to do it on something like the Greek gods or King Arthur or the lost continent of Atlantis.

This made her unpopular, for the teachers at Erebus did not like imagination; they liked neat handwriting. So they gave Iris lots of detentions, to shake the dreamer out of her.

Today was her worst class: double-period Social Studies. Since it was the very last class on Friday, Iris thought of it as a dragon guarding the gates to the weekend. Before entering the classroom, she imagined putting on a suit of armor and taking a magical sword in hand. Then she stepped in to face the foe.

Like most of her teachers, Mr. Pedlow was slightly insane. He was a direct descendant of General Robert E. Lee, and he mentioned this at least once a period. He had covered his desk with a large Confederate flag and an actual Civil War cannon that pointed directly at the students. For the last month, he had been making them copy out the Declaration of Independence onto graph paper. Iris hadn't gotten very far, because whenever she got to the part about "the pursuit of Happiness," her mind began to wander. The pursuit of Happiness was a nice thing to think about.

Mr. Pedlow bellowed, "Faster! I want to see the whole thing copied out by the end of the day, including the signatures!"

Iris had discovered that if she stared at the graph paper long enough, whatever she looked at afterward would be covered with a grid of tiny orangey lines. She would have to ask her mother why that happened. Iris looked out the window and covered the parking lot with the orange lines, which she imagined were an advanced security system, put in place to protect her, the princess, from assassins. The man with the mop, who seemed to be the school janitor, was really a ninja sent by an enemy king. She was watching him try to infiltrate the defenses, when Mr. Pedlow caught her eye. Iris panicked and looked back at her paper, but it was too late. She had violated one of her own rules for survival at Erebus: Never make eye contact.

"Iris Greenwold is off in dreamland again, I see. Are we keeping you from something, Miss Greenwold?" He studied her through his monocle.

"No, sir, Mr. Pedlow." She began to copy furiously.

"Dreaming up new tofu recipes?" The class snickered. Iris's mother worked at a tofu factory and had insisted on doing a presentation for Career Day. Iris had never heard the end of it.

"No, Mr. Pedlow." She hunched down in her seat and tried her best to look invisible, praying he wouldn't give her another detention.

He dipped an old-fashioned pen into ink and wrote something in his grade book. "That's one detention for you, written with a fountain pen once used by my ancestor Robert E. Lee. I advise you to pay more attention, Iris. I see that this is your eighth detention this year. Two more and you'll go to the principal."

Iris shivered. Strange tales were told about the principal of Erebus Middle School. She returned to her graph paper and copied steadily until the end of class, trying not to think about Happiness.

Chapter 2

Iris woke up Saturday morning to the strange and delicious smell of bacon. For a moment she was confused, and then it hit her. *My birthday!* It was the only day all year that her mother cooked meat that wasn't made of soy.

Iris curled up on her side and gloated. Presents and bacon! Of course, she reminded herself, the presents were bound to be disappointing. She looked at her bookshelf, where past gifts lay beneath a thick layer of dust: from her mother, an Albert Einstein lunch box that would have spelled endless teasing if brought to school, a dead Chia Pet, and a book called *Healing with Soy*; from her father, various dreidels, a twelve-volume *Illustrated History of the Jewish People,* and some stale chocolate coins. This year would probably bring more of the same, she thought. But she was wrong. There were magical things waiting to happen to Iris Greenwold. They had been waiting ever since she was born, and they were getting impatient.

"Yoo-hoo? Birthday girl?" Dr. Helen Greenwold blew into the room, brandishing a container of wheat germ. "Happy birthday, sweetie! Just think, twelve years and nine months ago, you were a zygote! I'm going to put a little wheat germ on that awful bacon, okay?"

"Mom, you can't!"

"It will counteract the carcinogens in the meat."

"I don't care. I like carsina . . . carsin . . . I like bacon. And I don't want that stuff on it, ruining it."

"Some millet porridge, then? I could put the wheat germ on that."

"All right, fine." If she argued, her mother might pull out a photo of a cancerous lung. "Did the mail come yet, Mom? I want to make sure I don't miss Dad's present."

"Don't be silly, Iris. It's only nine o'clock!"

But just then, the doorbell rang. Iris leaped out of bed and pressed the buzzer. When no one came up the steps, she went downstairs to check. She stood on the concrete stoop a moment, blinking in the morning sunshine. The parking lot was empty, except for a lone boy on a skateboard, skidding away over the asphalt. *He's up early,* Iris thought. There on the stoop, an inch from her bare feet, was a brown paper package, addressed to:

Iris Greenwold
Happy Asphalt Apartments #H-6
Middleville, Pennsylvania 19050

That was strange. UPS usually brought packages up the stairs. Iris bounded back to the breakfast table with her gift. Even though she expected to be disappointed, Iris still liked the feeling of suspense as she unwrapped the package, and liked knowing that whatever was inside was just for her. She set aside the Bubble Wrap, to pop later. Underneath was a thick hardcover book called *Bulfinch's Mythology*. She leafed through it with surprise. It was filled with stories about the Greek gods and had beautiful line drawings of heroes and monsters.

"Wow, Mom, look!" Iris said, her voice full of wonder. "I can't believe it. Dad actually got me something cool for a change. It's perfect."

"And it doesn't have to do with religion," her mother said drily. "Good for him. Maybe he's branching out."

"I guess I should call and thank him."

A pall settled over the room.

"Good idea," said her mother. "Call him quick and get it over with."

Iris sighed and picked up the phone. Calling her father was something dreadful that she had to do about every six months, like going to the dentist. Her parents had been divorced since she was one year old. She hardly ever saw her father, who lived in Wisconsin with his perpetually ill wife.

"Shabbat shalom, Iris!" he answered. "I don't normally answer the phone on the Jewish holy day, but I knew it would be you. Happy birthday. Guess what! LuAnne got over the shingles! Now we think she has some kind of liver fluke, which are small parasites that lodge in your liver and reproduce."

"I'm sorry to hear that."

"And her lung collapsed again. She describes it as a sort of dull, throbbing ache in the chest."

"I'm sorry to hear that."

As her father described the results of his wife's latest spinal tap, Iris's heartbeat accelerated and her eyes began to dart around the room. Conversations with her father induced the same panic response that a rat feels when backed into a corner. Had they been speaking face-to-face, she might have bitten him.

"And this may come as a big surprise, Iris, but it's her *ascending* colon that's giving her trouble these days! The *descending* colon is all sorted out now! We're thinking about starting her on a new treatment using medicinal leeches."

"I'm sorry to hear that." Iris picked up a pencil and began to draw a sketch of her stepmother covered in leeches. "So, I called to say thanks for the book, Dad. I love it."

"You're very welcome, Iris. I figured you should have your own copy. After all, it's the most important book in the world."

"Really? Wow, I didn't know you felt that way about those old stories, Dad."

"Those aren't just *old stories,* Iris. Those stories are the foundation of our civilization. And the poetry! Ah, it's the most beautiful poetry in the world."

"Yeah, it looks really good. I can't wait to get started reading it."

"Well, surely you've read it before!"

"No."

"That mother of yours! Doesn't she teach you anything about your heritage?"

"Um." Iris felt a bit confused. "Mom's not really into mythology and stuff like that."

From across the room, Iris's mother snorted and gestured with a Bunsen burner. "Is he starting in about religion again? Tell him we are atheists, Iris! I'm not filling your head with that crap. Tell him man created God, not the other way around!"

"Okay, Mom."

Iris's father said, "Ask your mother if she was there when God divided the heavens from the earth and told the ocean, 'Thus far shall you go and no farther.' Tell her the Lord created man, not the other way around!"

"Okay, Dad." Iris was used to her parents' skirmishes. It was hard to imagine them ever being married.

"And don't call it mythology, Iris. Every word in that book is true."

"Um, okay." Iris glanced at the cover of the book, which had a drawing of a winged horse and a snake-haired woman.

"Have you thought at all about going to synagogue, Iris? They have wonderful programs for young people of your age: hayrides, sing-alongs, dances!"

"Thanks, Dad. I'll think about that." The doorbell rang again, which was a good excuse to get off the phone. "Um, okay. Well, that's the doorbell, so I'd better go," Iris said, pressing the buzzer. "Thanks again. Tell LuAnne I say hi and that I'm sorry about the leeches. Bye!" Iris hung up and opened the door. She gazed in astonishment at the UPS man standing there.

"For Iris Greenwold," he said, and handed her a package, which bore her father's return address. Inside was a brand-new Bible.

Iris held the Bible in one hand and *Bulfinch's Mythology* in the other. She looked from one to the other in confusion. None of it made any sense. When she went back over the morning's phone conversation, it was clear that her father had been talking about the Bible the whole time. And there was no one else who sent her presents; she had no friends and no relatives who sent birthday gifts. So, if her father had not sent her the first book, *who had?*

If you listened very carefully right then, you might have heard a tiny sound in the air, about as loud as the air beneath a butterfly's wing. It was the sound of the things that were waiting to happen finally happening.

Chapter 3

Iris pulled the quilt up over her head to shut out the world. She always did her best thinking in bed. She opened *Bulfinch's Mythology* and shone her flashlight on the card pasted on the inside cover. "To Iris, on the occasion of her twelfth birthday. Knowledge is power." The card had a small drawing of an owl on the bottom.

As she studied the box the gift had come in, she noticed something she hadn't before: There was no stamp on the package, and no return address. Where the postage should have been, there was a rubber-stamp mark in the shape of a turtle. It must have been hand delivered.

Iris lay down on her back and shone the flashlight up at the underside of her quilt, which was covered with words written in metallic gold marker. They were Iris's ideas for dreams. Some were complete sentences, like *Travel back in time and save Joan of Arc,* and some were just words that she found exciting, like *Mount Olympus* or *Valkyries* or *firebird.* It didn't really work, telling herself what to dream about, but it was fun to try. The flashlight fell on one of her favorite dreams: *I am really the child of royalty (or fairies) and when I turn sixteen they come back to claim me.*

The golden letters glittered at her. It had always been her favorite thing to imagine that she wasn't really her parents' child but was actually someone magical and special. Then it wouldn't matter that she lived in a tiny apartment or went to an awful school where nobody liked her. It would all be a funny joke once her real family came to claim her.

Of course, Iris reminded herself, *I look an awful lot like my mother.* She reached up to hold the pendant her mother had given her that morning. It was actually a good present for a change: a piece of amber with a little fossilized bee inside, set on a gold chain. The stone felt warm in Iris's hand. *I love my mom,* Iris thought, and she felt a tiny bit guilty. *I don't really want to be someone else's daughter.*

But her father was a different story. . . .

She looked at the mythology book. Whoever sent it to her might have left some kind of clue inside. She curled up on her side and turned to chapter 1. It was a grown-up book, and Iris found it a bit difficult:

The religions of ancient Greece and Rome are extinct. The so-called divinities of Olympus have not a single worshipper among living men. They belong now not to the department of theology, but to those of literature and taste. There they still hold their place, and will continue to hold it, for they are too closely connected with the finest productions of poetry and art, both ancient and modern, to pass into oblivion.

Then Iris's eyes widened, for someone had written in the margin, in tiny block letters: DIDN'T YOU EVER WONDER, IRIS, WHAT HAPPENS TO GODS WHEN PEOPLE STOP WORSHIPPING THEM? WHERE DO THEY GO? WHAT DO THEY DO?

That was all the note said. Iris turned the pages eagerly, looking for more notes in the margin. A few pages later, she found one. This sentence in the book had been underlined: "The abode of the gods was on the summit of Mount Olympus, in Thessaly." Next to it, the same person had written: TOO CONSPICUOUS, NOWADAYS.

Iris continued to skim through the book, her mind racing with excitement. Certainly if someone wanted to hide away from the world, Middleville, Pennsylvania, would be a good place to do it, since nothing very exciting ever happened there. What if the Greek gods were alive and well and living in her town?

Iris spent almost the whole day in bed, poring over the book, looking for more clues. When she ate lunch and dinner, she took the book with her to the table. It was long, and sometimes she forgot all about the clues, since the stories themselves were so good. There were beautiful nymphs and princesses, dashing heroes, and—best of all—the gods, with all their different personalities and powers. When

Helen came into her room to say good night, Iris was still reading, and she continued until so late in the night that her eyelids ached to close.

At about two in the morning, she found what she was looking for.

Chapter 4

"The shore! Honey, it's freezing. Nobody goes to the shore in April! What would you do there?"

"I don't know. I just kind of want to walk around. You know, explore." Iris got nervous. What if her mother wouldn't take her? "We're doing a unit on oceanography in science . . ." Iris hated to lie, but it was for a good cause. "And I think it would be really helpful if I could do some firsthand observation of the ocean ecosystem to, you know, inspire my research?"

Helen regarded her daughter through thick spectacles. It was the same gaze she gave to a sick seedling. "Iris, honey, this is quite unlike you. Have you been getting enough sunlight and water?"

"I'm fine, Mom. I'm just taking more initiative. Please? It's my *birthday weekend.*"

Her mother looked skeptical, but she consented, with one condition: "The thing is, Iris, I have this presentation due Monday on my new soybean techniques. So if I take you, you're on your own. I'll sit in the car and work."

Iris smiled. That would be perfect. It would leave her all alone to find Poseidon. "That would be perfect, Mom. That would leave me all alone with the ocean ecosystem."

Her mother loaded a laptop computer, a chemistry set, seven Bunsen burners, and some DNA sequencing gel into the backseat of their Nissan Sentra. Iris took her backpack. In about an hour, they were in Margate, New Jersey.

The clue had been written so faintly that Iris had almost missed it. In a section titled "The Water Deities," this entry was circled:

[Neptune] was the chief of the water deities. The symbol of his power was the trident, or spear with three points, with which he used to shatter rocks, to call forth or subdue storms, to shake the shores and the like. He created the horse and was the patron of horse races. His own horses had brazen hooves and golden manes. They drew his chariot over the sea, which became smooth before him, while the monsters of the deep gamboled about his path.

Beside it, Iris's mysterious guide had written: SEEK POSEIDON AT THE GATE OF THE SEA. That was all it said, and though she stayed up several more hours skimming through the rest of the book, Iris had found no more of the strange notes.

Iris had also looked all over the Web for a place called the gate of the sea before it hit her: The boardwalk she had gone to all her life was in Margate, and *mar* means "sea" in Spanish. The book was just telling her to look in Margate! Sure enough, information listed two Poseidons in Margate, both business listings: Poseidon's Clam Shack and Poseidon's Taffy Hut. Iris could hardly believe it. It didn't seem possible that one of these could actually be the great Poseidon, god of the ocean. But she had carefully written down the addresses, and while her mother waited in the car and examined soybean slides, Iris set off to find her god.

Everything was pink inside the Taffy Hut, including the owner, a wrinkly old lady who gave a start when she heard the door jingle open. She slowly set down the book she was reading, a romance called *Baron of Desire.* The cover showed two kissing people riding through a deep stream on a horse.

"A customer! Welcome! We don't get many customers in April. Here, raspberry."

Iris popped the pink taffy into her mouth. "Mmm. Very good." It was.

"Contains actual ocean water! We are the preeminent taffy hut on the shore, and we stay open year-round even though it's a losing proposition. But I can't bear to close. What if someone is lovesick, abandoned by an arrogant baron? We have a duty to soothe sorrow with our toothsome taffy. Isn't that right, Poseidon?"

"Poseidon?" Iris couldn't believe it. On her first stop!

"Yes. Go say hi, Poseidon. That's it! Go say hi to the little lady."

A fluffy white poodle in a pink sweater trotted out from behind the counter.

"Oh. Poseidon's a poodle," Iris said. She bent down to pet him, but he bared his teeth and snarled.

"Poseidon! Bad boy! Sorry about that, love; he's just depressed because business is so slow. So, what brings you to the shore on a day like this?"

"Oh, I was just coming to meet someone."

"Ooo!" The woman clapped her hands. "A romance! I love romances! Are you very sad? Has he double-crossed you? What's his name, dear?"

"Well, it's kind of a secret. No offense. It's just—"

The woman nodded knowingly. "No offense taken. I understand the importance of discretion in these matters. Poseidon, as well, is very discreet, silent as the tomb." The dog wagged his tail. "And it's not for want of women, believe me! He has quite a history with the blond cocker spaniels at the chowder place." She lowered her voice to a whisper. *"There have been puppies."*

Iris thought the woman was almost crazy enough to teach at Erebus. "Um, can I have a small box of the assorted taffy, please?"

"Yum!" said her mom when Iris dropped the taffy off back at the car. "Tons of refined sugar, of course, but I suppose we can treat ourselves. This was a terrific idea, Iris. We should come to the shore more often. I'm getting a lot of work done. I think this is going to be the best presentation I've ever given. Maybe I'll even be promoted."

"That's great, Mom! Well, I'm off to do some more research."

"Okay, honey. Meet me back at the car in exactly two hours."

"Okay, Mom."

"If you get lost, go to that big lighthouse over there, and I'll come to find you."

"Okay, Mom."

"Don't get lost. Exactly two hours."

"*Okay,* Mom. *Jeez.*"

But Iris's mom was right. Whenever your parents let you go off on your own to look for mythological figures, you should always agree upon a meeting place beforehand. Don't pick something that might move, like a sand dune or a bookmobile. Pick something large and permanent, like a lighthouse.

Iris did not get lost, because the boardwalk was under her feet the whole time. She saw no one as she walked except for one stray dog dragging a huge piece of driftwood. It was a wonderful feeling to be all alone on the boardwalk, just her and the ocean. Iris inhaled deeply, delighting at the scent of salt. She felt swept clean by the sea air, as if it were blowing right through her. By the time she reached Poseidon, she was skipping.

Chapter 5

The clam shack was dilapidated and empty, with a neon sign that flickered a few times and went out. There was a bell on the counter, but when Iris rang it no one came. A lone seagull looked up at her, then went back to pecking at a kaiser roll. Iris trudged around the side of the building, past the Dumpsters with their reek of fish. Then she saw him.

Poseidon stood behind his restaurant, knee-deep in the ocean. His head drooped with the weight of his beard, and his broad shoulders hunched beneath his overcoat. Never before had Iris seen longing like his. He gazed at the sea like it was every good thing that has ever gone missing. "Hello," Iris said. He looked up at her, then back at the sea.

"They don't listen to me anymore," he said.

"Who?"

"The Nereids, the sirens, the mermaids, the fish, the waves, the water. The water doesn't listen to me anymore." A tear rolled down the side of his face and fell into the surf. Iris felt awful. This wasn't at all how she had pictured Poseidon.

"What's a Nereid?"

"Nereids are like mermaids, only more beautiful. They used to follow me around, singing. But now they're all gone."

"Where did they go?"

"I don't know," he said. "Probably somewhere nicer."

"And where are all the other gods?" Iris asked.

"Oh, hanging around."

"Hanging around the shore?" Iris looked around her, just in case.

"No. Only I am at the shore. They're just, you know, hanging around Philadelphia. We choose the place that makes us feel comfortable."

"And—are the other gods . . ." Iris didn't know how to ask her question in a polite way.

"Are they all as pathetic as me?"

"No! I didn't mean that. But you do seem really sad."

"I know. It's what happens to us before we die." Poseidon gazed out over the sea.

"But I thought you were immortal!"

"We're immortal as long as we keep eating ambrosia and drinking nectar. But if we get really sad and lose our appetites, we die."

"But why are you so sad, Poseidon? If I were a god, I'd be happy."

He sighed. "Immortality isn't all it's cracked up to be. The world moves on and leaves you behind."

Iris had a hard time believing him. She imagined being able to live through the ages. She would be able to learn so much. She could learn every language in the world, play every instrument, meet all the famous people throughout time.

"Immortality stinks," he said, another tear rolling down his face and hanging from the end of his nose. "I am at low tide, Iris. Low tide."

"But don't the other gods come and cheer you up?"

He shook his head. "They've got their own problems. I don't see the other gods much, since we got to Philadelphia. Everyone pretty much keeps to themselves."

"I know how it feels to be lonely, Poseidon." Then a strange thought occurred to her. "You called me by my name, but I never told it to you."

"I knew you were coming. Gods know things." He was silent again and looked back out to sea. "Schools of fish used to dance for me. The squid moved its tentacles in patterns only I knew. And Amphitrite used to go with me everywhere." He broke down into sobs.

"Oh Poseidon," said Iris, and she put her hand on his shoulder.

As if her touch had given him strength, Poseidon stood up straighter and threw back his shoulders. "Look at me," he said, wiping his nose on a cuff. "What kind of god am I, letting you stand out here hungry and cold, while I mope. I have an idea: oysters for lunch! Oysters always cheer you up." He motioned to Iris to follow him as he trudged up the hill toward the restaurant.

Chapter 6

"Well, I don't know. I've never eaten an oyster before." Iris watched Poseidon open the oysters. He worked with incredible dexterity, prying apart the two halves of craggy shell and scraping the slimy gray insides into a bowl. They were standing in the kitchen of the clam shack, surrounded by piles of napkins that said KING OF THE SEA, sacks full of tartar sauce packets, and mounds of toothpicks shaped like tridents.

"Then, you have to try them. They are one of the great delicacies of the ocean." He lifted one to his lips and slurped it up, raw. "Thousands of years ago, I invented the pearl to impress a Nereid named Amphitrite. By accident, I also invented the oyster. That's what you call a happy accident!"

"What happened to Amphitrite?" Iris asked.

"We got married, but it didn't last. She said I was stifling her creativity. Ran off to live the bohemian life, and I lost track of her. I miss her. It's lonely here."

Iris decided to change the subject, so she asked Poseidon if she could see his trident. She had read many myths in *Bulfinch's Mythology* that mentioned Poseidon's mighty three-pronged staff. But this made him even sadder.

"It's over there," he said, and pointed to what Iris had taken for a coatrack.

She could hardly bear to look. Covered with dust, rusty in places, the trident gave no hint of its former glory. A broken piñata hung from one of its prongs; an old boot swung from another. The center prong was free, and Iris could tell, from the pile of caps ringing the base, that he was using it to open soda bottles. Iris didn't know what to say. She began to understand what Poseidon had meant when he said that immortality was not all it was cracked up to be.

"And that thing next to it," said Poseidon, pointing to a monolithic steel machine, "that's the Frialator. It gets the oysters perfectly crunchy outside, and warm and steamy inside." He tossed the oysters into a bowl of bread crumbs and shook the bowl around so everything arced up into the air and landed back in place. Then he bellowed, "TAKE COVER!"

Iris ducked behind a large ball of aluminum foil.

"DROPPING OYSTERS!" Poseidon hurled the oysters through the air. They landed with a fizz in the Frialator, as hot oil shot up and hit the ceiling. "Not bad, huh?" he said, motioning to Iris to get up.

"Yeah. But why don't you just put them in with a spoon or something? That seems kind of dangerous."

"Oh, in the old days, I used to have Amphitrite working in here with me. Sometimes I still clown around the way I used to when she was here." He looked down at the floor and shuffled a booted foot back and forth over the peeling linoleum. A timer rang. "Ah. The oysters are ready. You can't cook an oyster too long." He shuffled over to the Frialator and did mysterious things. Then he handed Iris a hot-dog bun in waxed paper.

Some people hate oysters, but these people are rarely important enough to appear in books. Iris thought the oyster roll was the most delicious thing she'd ever eaten. The hot-dog bun was warm and crisp, its insides coated with butter and tartar sauce. The oysters were creamy and salty and crunchy, all at the same time.

"Poseidon, this is awesome!"

The old man smiled sadly. "Thank you. It's nice to have someone to share it with."

"Poseidon, someone sent me a book in the mail. That's how I found out you were here."

"I know."

"But who sent the book, Poseidon, and why?"

"Why she sent it to you, I do not know. No one tells me anything. And as for who sent it—well, if she didn't sign it, I'm not sure I should tell you. I mean, maybe she wants it to stay a surprise. But she did call me this morning. Said you'd be dropping by. And told me to tell you this story."

Poseidon set aside his spatula and stood up to his full

height. With the first words, his voice became deep and rhythmic as the sea. The story was an old one, of the days when he was king.

Iris had so many questions to ask him. She did not understand why all of this was happening, and why it was happening to *her* in particular. She had no idea why he was telling her this particular myth. But she knew there must be some kind of message in it for her, so she listened carefully.

Chapter 7

*Back when the ocean was alive and gods walked the earth,
there lived a mortal king named Ceyx. He was a good king, as
kings go. He didn't deserve to die, but who does, really? It's just
the way the tides roll, Iris. The big fish eat the little ones.*

*Ceyx ruled in peace for many years with his wise queen
Halcyone and their little son. But one day, King Ceyx prepared to set sail on a long voyage. In those days, sea voyages
were perilous things, far more than they are today. The ocean
seethed with spirits: sirens, Nereids, sea gods large and small,
and me, Poseidon the trident-shaker, mightiest of them all.*

*Ceyx's wife saw it coming. She begged her husband not to go
on the trip, begged him to take her and the boy with him. She
cried and screamed for days, but Ceyx would not listen. Ships
are no place for women and children, he argued. Plus, if the
trip was dangerous, why should all of them be endangered?*

He soothed his wife's tears and left, promising to return in three months' time. Halcyone was forlorn.

Have you ever watched dogs tied up outside a store? The dog stares into the store, not understanding why the master has deserted them. Sometimes the dog strains against the leash; sometimes it barks miserably; sometimes it trembles. Dogs' hearts are so eager that they cannot bear separation, not even for five minutes. Halcyone loved her husband with a dog's love, and dog love is deep.

Halcyone set up an altar to Hera in her bedroom, and she offered prayers to the goddess every day for her husband's safe return. Hera was the patroness of faithful wives. She smiled to see Halcyone's devotion and came to me to request that I guide the man's ship safely over the waters.

It was too late. I do not enjoy wrecking ships; it's just part of my job. I have quotas to fill. King Ceyx had died bravely and quickly, calling out Halcyone's name. I told this to Hera.

Halcyone's earnest prayers, which had given Hera so much pleasure, were now torture to hear. Every evening the lonely queen bowed her head and prayed for her dead husband, "Dear Goddess Hera, protect my brave and wonderful husband. Let not even the slightest harsh wind hit the sails of the ship. And keep the other sailors safe, too, so that they may return to their wives and families. Please keep him full of love for me, as I am full of love for him. Goddess Hera, you are loyal and merciful. Smile on me and mine."

When she had watched three full moons come and go, Halcyone became anxious. She prayed more often, begging the goddess to speed her husband's ship home. Finally, Hera couldn't bear it anymore. She called for her messenger, the lovely, fleet-footed Iris.

"Yay, Iris is in the story!" Iris blurted out. Then she felt bad for interrupting. "I'm sorry, Poseidon, it's just, I never knew there was a goddess with my name until I read about her last night, and the Bulfinch book hardly said anything about her. I would like to meet her more than anything! The goddess of the rainbow!" But Poseidon only shook his head sadly.

"She was one of the first goddesses to die. Faded away just like her rainbow. I think she was tired of living, to tell you the truth. Hera was a tough mistress, always bossing her around, making her spy on Zeus and his girlfriends."

Iris traveled by sliding down the rainbow. She wore a multicolored gown made of raindrops, and wherever grace and speed were needed, we called on her. Hera told Iris that she needed a message carried to Somnus, the god of sleep.

"Tell him to send his son Morpheus, the one who is so skillful at assuming human forms and voices, to Queen Halcyone tonight in her sleep. Let the queen dream that she sees her husband, not as he looked when he left, but as he looks now: bruised, sea-tossed. Let him say that he died loving her and calling out her name. For I can no longer bear to hear this woman's futile prayers. Go now, Iris, be swift."

Iris turned to go. Her water-bead dress swirled around her, sending up a spray of dew. She unrolled her rainbow shawl and said:

"Πυρρός

Σανδαράκινος

Ξανθός

Χλωρός

Ὑακίνθινος

Πορφύρεος

Ἰοειδής"

When she spoke these words, the shawl became a real rainbow, arcing up into the sky. But it was a special rainbow that
would take Iris wherever she wanted to go.

"The entrance gates to the house of the sleep lord!" she
yelled out. "Seven clouds west of the Great Bear." She jumped
on. The next moment, she was facing the sleeping lions that
guarded Somnus's palace. She stopped to pat them between the
ears, and they nuzzled her hand in their sleep. She stepped
through the gates. Inside, the halls were full of snoring servants
and quiet harp music. All the windows were covered with
heavy purple velvet, and so she made her way by candlelight to
the king's chamber. Somnus was in bed. He noticed the bright
goddess and inclined his head. Somnus was very handsome.
His hair stood out from his head in dark tangled locks, and his
gray eyes were glazed with dreams.

Iris bent over him and whispered in his ear, "Gentlest of the
gods, lord of sleep, I come to ask a favor of you in Hera's name."

The king nodded and moved over to make room for Iris in the
bed. He patted the white sheets. "Join me . . . It's . . . nap time."

It was hard for Iris to resist; the bed looked so soft and sweet.
The king smelled like down blankets. He smelled like warm

milk. Iris's head began to droop on her neck, and she longed to curl up beside him.

She shook her head and said, "Thank you, but I must remember my errand. Hera desires that you send your son Morpheus to Queen Halcyone tonight in the guise of her slain husband, Ceyx. Have him tell the queen he died with her name on his lips."

King Somnus yawned widely and said, "Okay . . . now . . . I . . . sleep again."

Iris stumbled back through the halls. Her eyelids felt heavy and her feet felt leaden. She threw wide the doors of the palace and walked back out into the sunlight. She unrolled her rainbow, then yelled out, "Home!"

That night, Halcyone had her nightmare. Morpheus wrapped himself up in Ceyx's form as easily as other men throw on a robe. Morpheus was a genius at impersonation. He could assume the voice and body of anyone so perfectly that he would fool their own mother.

As a child, he used to play all kinds of tricks on us. I remember once Ares had built a marble statue of himself for the Spartans' war temple. It was magnificent: twenty feet high, brutal, and warlike. While Ares admired the workmanship, Morpheus hid in the bushes outside the temple and thundered, "HEAR ME, I AM MIGHTY ZEUS! THAT STATUE DOES NOT PLEASE ME AT ALL! PAINT IT PINK. BRIGHT PINK. WITH LITTLE PURPLE UNICORNS ALL OVER IT." Ares was furious, but what could he do? Zeus had spoken.

Needless to say, the statue looked ludicrous covered in

purple unicorns, though Aphrodite liked it. When Ares found out the voice had been Morpheus's, he had murder on his mind. Zeus thought it was funny, and he protected the boy. But to appease Ares, Zeus decreed that from then on, Morpheus's powers would be limited. He would be able to take other forms and voices only in the world of dreams.

Halcyone smiled in her sleep as her beloved husband approached her. The likeness was perfect. As he embraced her, however, she smelled the sea on him. They kissed and her mouth filled with water. She pulled back and looked at him. There was seaweed in his hair, and barnacles on his cheeks. His voice was full of salt.

"Beloved," the dream-image said, "I come to tell you to give up false hopes. My last thought was of you. Good-bye."

Halcyone's screams woke the whole palace. She could not be comforted. She ran out from the palace and down to the seashore, wailing. From my underwater castle, I watched her run weeping to the shore. I washed her husband's body up on shore at that moment. Halcyone fell to her knees on the beach and held Ceyx's limp form. Her cries broke my heart.

Soon Halcyone embraced her husband with wings, not arms. Her lamentation turned to birdsong. Beneath her, Ceyx's crumpled body shrunk and grew feathers. He stood up on spindly legs, shook off the sand, and hurled himself upward. She followed. I made them kingfishers, which is why those birds have sorrowful cries and always mate for life. Ceyx and Halcyone climbed through the sky in widening spirals, together again at last.

Chapter 8

After Poseidon finished the story, he lay down on the floor, in a fetal position, with his head on a sack of oyster crackers. "Go away, Iris. I want to be alone. That story makes me sad."

"But, Poseidon, can't you tell me where to find the other gods? Or who sent me the book?"

"All people care about these days is themselves," he said. "I told you a nice, tragic story and made you special oysters, and now all you want is to get more information out of me."

Iris hung her head. She felt ashamed of herself. Here he was, curled up on the dirty floor, and all she could think about was her own adventures. "I'm sorry, Poseidon. Really I am. It's just that I'm so excited about finding out that gods exist and there's so much I want to know. I'm very grateful to you for lunch and for the story. It was a beautiful story. Thank you."

"You're welcome." He closed his eyes.

"Poseidon, are you going to be okay? Isn't there anything I can do for you?"

He grunted. "I haven't been okay since Amphitrite left, but there's nothing you can do about that. Things change, life goes on. Go, your mother will be worried."

Iris looked at the starfish clock on the wall. He was right; it had already been two hours. She bent down and gently kissed Poseidon's cheek. He smelled like salt. "Thank you again." *And I* am *going to help you,* she added silently. *I'm going to find a way.* "Good-bye, Poseidon."

He did not answer. Iris found it hard to leave him, but she had to. She ran back to the car, where her mother was visible in the backseat, bent over her laptop. Helen looked up when Iris knocked on the window.

"Iris! Is it time already? It seems like you just left."

"I know, Mom. Time flies when you're having fun."

"And nothing's more fun than science," Helen said, showing Iris the chart she had made. "See, I show the history of soybean hybridization through the ages." She scrolled down to the next page. "And here's my new technique, and I even made a pie chart of how much money it could save our factory!"

"That's great, Mom."

Helen started up the car and they headed back toward the New Jersey turnpike, leaving Poseidon behind. Iris leaned her head against the window and watched the beach go by. The sun was setting into the water, turning it gold. *Such a long day,* Iris reflected, *and so many questions* . . .

Before she knew it, she was asleep, waking only when they pulled up in front of the apartments.

"Hey, sleepyhead," her mother said. "Looks like your dad sent you another package."

Iris sat up with a start. "What?"

"Another package for you, on the stoop. That's weird, I didn't think UPS delivered on Sundays."

Iris scooped up the parcel before her mother could see that it had no return address or that there was a picture of a turtle where the stamp should be. Across the parking lot, a skinny boy on a skateboard watched Iris pick up the package. He grinned and sped off into the evening.

Chapter 9

Inside the box was a beautiful woven shawl, in all the colors of the rainbow. The shawl had a label with a picture of an owl on one side and MADE BY HAND. DRY-CLEAN ONLY. on the other. Now she understood why Poseidon had told her *that particular* myth. She fingered the fine cloth lovingly.

Was it possible? Would it work?

Iris was bad at remembering the kinds of things you get tested on at school, like dates and names and countries, but she was extremely good at remembering anything made up or magical. If there were a Standardized Imagination Test, she would have been in the top percentile.

And this is why she remembered the spell perfectly:

"Πυρρός
Σανδαράκινος

Ξανθός
Χλωρός
῾Υακίνθινος
Πορφύρεος
᾽Ιοειδής"

Iris's tiny bedroom filled with shimmering prismatic light. She looked down and saw that her clothing had disappeared. In its place was a dress made out of water. It was so beautiful that Iris held her breath. The waterdrops were held together with a net of silver thread, and each drop shimmered with a different color of the rainbow. Iris spun around and it swirled, sending up a spray of mist that hung in the air. She laughed for joy.

The cloth shawl had turned into an arc of light that stretched from her feet up into the ceiling and seemed to shoot right through the roof and into the sky. Iris was thankful she lived on the top floor. She set one foot on the end of the rainbow. It was cool and slippery, like a big slide. She closed her eyes and sat down on the end. She could go anywhere at all now.

But she didn't know where any of the other gods lived.

"Take me to whoever is sending me these gifts."

Nothing happened. The rainbow seemed to be waiting for more information. Maybe if she gave it a proper name? She thought she'd go right to the top.

"Take me to Zeus!"

But again nothing happened. Iris frowned. Maybe the rainbow could only take her somewhere she knew?

"Take me to Poseidon."

At once she heard the immense sound of waves. There was a brief feeling of dizziness and falling through space, and then she landed on her butt on the cold sand, and the rainbow landed in a heap beside her, cloth again. Her water-bead dress had reverted back to jeans and a T-shirt. Iris jumped up, grinning. It worked! She could go anywhere now!

She looked up at the back of the clam shack. It was dark and quiet. Nearby was a man, curled up in a fetal position, next to a huge sand sculpture. She ran over, worried. It was Poseidon. He was snoring peacefully, but his cheeks were stained with tears.

The sand sculpture showed Poseidon as he must have looked in his youth, riding on a shark, with his trident in one hand. He had huge muscles and long flowing hair. He wore a great jeweled crown. Around the waves at his feet, dolphins played and mermaids sang. Poseidon had decorated the sculpture with starfish, mussel shells, and Coke bottle caps. Iris shook her head and turned back to the thin old man curled up on the sand. It was hard to believe he had ever been the king of the sea.

She brushed some sand from his beard.

"I'll help you if I can, Poseidon. I promise." *But first,* she thought, *I'll have to find out where the other gods are. Maybe something will happen to show me the way.* She shook out the shawl and spoke the Greek words again. The rainbow arced up into the night sky and out over the ocean. Iris gasped. It was even more beautiful here than it had been in her bedroom. She stepped on the edge and whispered, "Take me back to bed."

When Helen peeked in her room five minutes later, Iris was fast asleep.

Chapter 10

The next day at school was torture, since all Iris could think about was getting home and doing research into the gods' whereabouts. She had decided that Zeus might be the owner of the big electrical power plant just over the border in Delaware, and she thought there was a chance that Ares, the god of war, ran the boxing gym in Philly that had those commercials with the bulldog in them. It was intolerable being cooped up in Erebus on a day when she had so much thinking and adventuring to do.

Her extra impatience made the day even worse than usual. Mr. Pedlow said she looked sullen, and he assigned her a five-page composition entitled "The South Shall Rise Again." Gym was traumatic and humiliating, and consisted of one long game of tag in which Iris was "it" the whole time. At lunch she found a strange piece of bone in her chicken potpie, and when she brought it to her biology class for identification, the teacher, crazy Mrs. Webb, actually gave her a detention.

That made nine detentions. One more and she would have to go to the principal. Iris resolved to be extra careful. She spent the detention writing her composition on the South, in which the Greek gods figured prominently, and she leaped up at the stroke of five. She had decided to go home via rainbow, and she sneaked out onto the blacktop behind the basketball courts.

No one was in sight, so Iris took out the shawl, summoned the rainbow, and stepped on.

"Happy Asphalt Apartments, please!" She was feeling just a bit proud of herself when she did this, almost as if she were the goddess Iris herself.

She landed in a heap of coffee grounds and banana peels.

"Hey, what the—"

She looked around and saw metal walls. It was the Dumpster outside her apartment complex. The shawl was safely draped over the side of the Dumpster, and Iris thought she could hear laughter. She held her nose and smiled.

"You've got a sense of humor, I see. I guess it serves me right."

The inside of a Dumpster is an interesting place, and Iris spent a moment looking around at the debris. It reminded her a bit of an archaeological site, with layers upon layers of evidence about civilization. As she picked her way to the opening, a letter caught her eye. It lay faceup, and Iris could hardly help reading it. After she had read it, she wished she hadn't.

Dear Dr. Helen Greenwold,

We at Tofu-licious are grateful for your twenty years of service in our soybean testing and development division.

We are sorry to inform you that you have been replaced by a robot that can perform your job approximately one thousand times faster than you.

We are enclosing a check for two weeks' pay. Have a nice day!

Warmest regards,

J. Norman Dweebe
CEO, Tofu-licious, Inc.

—HUNGRY FOR A CHANGE? TRY TOFU-LICIOUS!—

Iris felt horrible. Not only had she violated her mother's privacy, but what she'd just learned was terribly sad. Her mother loved her job. And what would they do for money now that she was out of work? Iris hurried up the steps and opened their door.

"Mom?"

"Hi, Iris. How was school?" Helen was watering the plants.

"It was great, Mom . . . How was your day?"

"Oh . . ." Her mother sighed and ran a finger down the rubber-tree trunk. "Well, I did my big presentation, but I don't think anybody cared."

"What happened, Mom?" Iris felt guilty asking a question she already knew the answer to.

Helen put down the watering can. Iris could tell she had been crying; her glasses were all foggy. "You know, Iris, I don't really feel like talking about it right now."

"That's okay, Mom. I understand. You know, your plants look beautiful. That rubber tree's really getting big. It looks like it could grow right through the ceiling."

Her mother nodded. "I was wondering if you'd do me a favor."

"Sure, Mom. Anything."

"Before it gets dark, can you run over to that used-record store—you know, the one in the strip mall? And can you see if they'll buy any of my old jazz records? I've got some really good ones. They're all in great condition. We should be able to get some money for them."

Her mother had set a pile of LPs on the sofa. It broke Iris's heart. The "record store" was CDs only; nobody wanted to buy old LPs in Middleville. But Iris didn't tell her mother that.

"Okay, Mom. I'll try."

"And don't let them talk you down, either. Those are good albums. One of them's even autographed." Her mother looked at the records sadly. "It's hard to give them up, but . . ." She shook her head. "They're just things; it doesn't matter. You get a good price for them, okay?"

"Sure, Mom."

"That's my girl."

Iris tucked them under her arm and headed out the door. "I love you, Mom."

"I love you, too, kiddo."

It was just a short walk to the Middleville strip mall, which featured an excellent fast-food restaurant, the Monster Burger, several vacant storefronts, and the Severed Head CD Shoppe. The proprietor of the Severed Head was a heavyset man wearing cleaver-shaped earrings and a T-shirt with BLOOD BATH across the front. He laughed at Iris's bag of LPs.

"We don't sell LPs, and we don't sell jazz."

Iris had known he was going to laugh at her, but it still felt lousy. "Yeah, I figured. Is there anywhere else I should try?"

"Around here? No. Nobody around here listens to that stuff. You might as well throw it out."

"All right, thanks." She turned to go, but he called her back.

"Wait a minute. Some guy came by a while ago with some flyers about a jazz show. Maybe you wanna check it out. Take those to the show, sell them there, or something. Now where did I put those flyers?"

He reached into the wastebasket, rooted around, and handed Iris a damp, beer-scented flyer. Her luck was changing.

···· FRESH, FLY, FUNKY ····
Live Music Seven Nights a Week
at DAPHNE'S TRUNK
Philadelphia's Last Real Jazz Club
2917 North Broad Street

Featuring: All the Happening Cats, Including
the Divine Sounds of Apollo, Tenor Saxophone

"A sound as bright as the sun."
–P. HYMNIA, *PHILADELPHIA INSPIRER*

SETS AT 9 AND 11 P.M. · NO SQUARES ALLOWED

Chapter 11

Iris waited for the sound of her mother's snores to seep through the thin wall of her bedroom. Then she spread the shawl out on the floor of her room and called out:

"Πυρρός
Σανδαράκινος
Ξανθός
Χλωρός
'Υακίνθινος
Πορφύρεος
'Ιοειδής"

The rainbow was the most beautiful thing Iris had ever seen. She looked at each of the neon-bright colors: red, orange, yellow, green, blue, indigo, and deepest violet.

Suddenly she understood what the spell meant. She was calling out their names, the names of the colors, in their own language. The rainbow flared up brighter for a moment, as if it rejoiced in her discovery.

A moment later, Iris stood in front of a doorway on a dark street in West Philadelphia. The door was outlined in white Christmas lights and painted all over with green leaves. She knocked, and it swung open.

"Welcome to the Trunk."

The man speaking to her was approximately eight feet tall. He was wearing a tank top with THUG on it and had a small tattoo of Earth on his shoulder. Cigarette smoke billowed around him. Iris coughed.

"Cover is twenty-five dollars, and that includes ten dollars toward your first drink. And I'll have to see some ID. You look underage."

"I'm twelve, and I only have about seven dollars." Iris looked around frantically for help, but the huge man blocked everything else from her view. Behind him she could hear the booming of drums, the deep growl of the bass, and, above them both, the pure, golden voice of Apollo's saxophone. The huge man laughed.

"Twelve? What are you doing out so late? You should be home in bed."

"Apollo is expecting me," she lied.

"Yeah, right," he said. "What's in the bag?"

"Some records I'm trying to sell."

"Let me see them." He took the bag from her and

shuffled through the records. "Hmm, not bad, not bad . . . I don't have this one . . . You an Ayler fan, huh?"

"Well, not really. It's my mom's. She asked me to sell it for her."

He put the LPs back in the bag and handed it to her. "Well, she has good taste."

Behind him, the club filled with applause. When it subsided, a silky voice yelled out, "Yo, Atlas, who's at the door?"

The huge man held her gaze and yelled back, "Some shorty. Says you're expecting her."

"Let her in, then."

Atlas shrugged. He stepped out of the way, revealing a dimly lit, low-ceilinged room that was hazy with cigarette smoke. Candles twinkled in the centers of tables, and people leaned over them to talk and kiss. Everybody was dressed up and having a fabulous time.

The stage was set back from the rest of the room. Three men were on it, and Iris knew from the power coming off him that the tall, thin one was Apollo. She realized with surprise that he was black. In fact, most of the people in the bar were black. This was a new experience for Iris, since pretty much everybody in Middleville was white. Apollo smiled at her, and she blushed. He was very, very handsome.

"About time, girl; the set started forty-five minutes ago!" He waved his arm to her, beckoning her up onstage. Then he turned to the audience. "Ladies and gentlemen, our vocalist has finally arrived. She's not very punctual, but—what can I say?—she's a genius." Iris shook her head, terrified. She could barely carry a tune.

"You're the singer? Jeez, you shoulda told me that! Go on," said Atlas, and he led her in.

Iris tried to explain that it was a mistake, but Atlas shook his head. "Don't be modest, sugar. Apollo says you're ready to sing, you're ready. He's not the type to flatter you just 'cause you're a girl." He put his hand on her arm and guided her through the maze of tables. The audience members nodded to her and smiled. Iris looked up at Apollo as she climbed the stage stairs and gasped. For a moment, his skin and eyes flashed a beautiful orange gold, and rays of light shone from his body. His saxophone turned into a huge golden bow and quiver of arrows. Then he went back to normal, and Iris thought it had just been her imagination. He winked at her, his eyes back to their deep blue black. And she heard a singsong voice in her head.

That was a hint of the old Apollo;
When I start to play, you follow.

Iris looked at him, shocked. He could communicate to her without speaking. Aloud, he said, "Ladies and gentlemen. Lovely ladies and lucky gentlemen, this is an important moment at Daphne's Trunk." Iris squinted out at the crowd over the stage lights, but it was hard to see. "Today we welcome one of the great up-and-coming jazz singers of the new generation to our stage."

"But Mr. Apollo," she whispered, "I'm not a singer. You must have me mixed up with someone. I'm kinda tone-deaf." He answered her, once again, soundlessly.

Don't worry, Iris, I know who you are.
News travels fast in this bar.

"Ladies and gents, I give you the mellifluous tones of Iris Greenwold!" The audience applauded warmly. Iris smiled. It felt good to have people applaud for her, even though she knew they would soon be booing her off the stage. Why was Apollo doing this? Did he want to put his nightclub out of business?

Apollo cued the drummer. Iris's palms began to sweat furiously. The bass entered, low, pounding in her stomach. Then Apollo played his saxophone. He played notes that felt like thick, polished bands of bronze. They hung in the air a long time, vibrating and shimmering before they disappeared.

She didn't know what to do, but she trusted Apollo. She drew a deep breath into her belly and leaned into the microphone. The drummer was watching her, grinning and nodding as he played.

The words came out of her mouth magically: "Let's take it back a little. Back before jazz was born. Way back in time to the days when gods walked the earth. This is a ballad about a boy named Phaëthon, son of the god Apollo and a mortal woman named Clymene. It goes a little something like this . . ."

Somehow Apollo knew how much Iris had always wished that her father were someone different, someone magical. And he was speaking through her, using the music. He was warning her with his own son's sad story.

Iris sang.

Chapter 12

Nobody knows the trouble I've seen;
Nobody knows the sorrow.
Be careful what you wish for, child;
Be careful what you borrow.

Every day Phaëthon played with his friends
In a glade by a babbling river.
They made-believe branches were arrows and bows
And an empty jar was the quiver.

Phaëthon always insisted he'd won
For his father was known for the bow.
"Another bull's-eye," he'd yell out with joy,
"It runs in the family, you know!"

One day his friends, who were all mortal-born,
Grew weary of losing this game,
And tired of hearing their arrogant friend
Brag of his father's great name.

"If Phoebus Apollo's your father," they jeered,
"Why doesn't he ever come by?
Or ever send presents or tokens or letters
Falling down out of the sky?"

He ran to his mother, who stared at the sun.
"Phaëthon, what more can I say?
Your birth is divine, and I swear it to you
By my love whom I see every day."

But Phaëthon needed assurance of this,
Some proof he could hold in his hand.
He was not content with the sight of the sun;
He needed to meet with the man.

He followed the sun where it set in the west,
Leaving his mother behind,
And as with the moth who flies into the flame,
He had only union in mind.

Fear and joy in equal amounts
Mingled in Phaëthon's soul
When he finally reached the doorway of brass
And entered the palace of gold.

But warmer than brass and brighter than gold
Was the voice that rang out from within:
"So, at last the lion cub comes to our door,
Seeking the den of his kin."

"The story your mother told you is true:
You are Clymene's and you are mine.
How else could your eyes be so Clymene-bright
And your smile so Apollo-divine?

"As proof of my love, I will give you a boon;
Speak and it shall be done.
Whatever you want I will give: This I swear
By the River Unkissed by the Sun."

Phaëthon raised his eyes to his father,
But the light was too much to bear,
For Apollo wore robes of sunbeams and platinum,
And emeralds dripped from his hair.

"Father, the boys I play with at school
Will never believe what I say
Unless they see me way up in the sky;
I want to be Sun for a day!"

Iris stopped while Apollo soloed. She could hear his pain
from the way he played. He was crying with the saxophone, mourning his son. The notes were like fountain
water, shooting up in the air and falling back down. It was

so beautiful that Iris didn't want it to stop, ever. She didn't want to have to sing anymore, to hear the end of the story. But then Apollo sped up and played hot, frenzied lines of notes, tying up the solo. The audience whooped. Apollo nodded to her, and she had to continue.

Apollo wept and shook his bright locks
Four times until golden sparks fell.
"My son, how bitterly do I regret
Having sworn on the river of hell.

"For breakfast my horses eat lava and eggs
With fresh-squeezed volcano juice.
No driver but me can handle their fire,
Not even Poseidon or Zeus."

But stupidly Phaëthon stopped up his ears
And stubbornly stuck to his prize,
So much did he crave the glory and fame
Of driving the sun through the skies.

At last Apollo said to the boy,
"I am forced to comply with your wish.
You are foolish, my son, and foolish was I
When I swore on Persephone's Styx.

"The heat will be fierce on your tender young skin,
This balm will buy you some time."

And he covered the boy with magical salve
That smelled of lilac and lime.

"Don't go too low or you'll blister the earth,
Too high or you'll damage the sky.
Hold the reins with all of your strength.
To drop them means you will die.

"The horses are Phlegon, Eous, and Aethon,
The fourth one's name is Pyrois.
If they start to go crazy, call out their names,
In a stern and masterful voice."

Phaëthon jumped on the chariot seat
And laughed at his friends on the earth:
"They'll be jealous to see me driving the sun!
They'll be sorry they questioned my birth!"

But the laughter froze on Phaëthon's lips
When the chariot started to roll;
The horses, distrusting the hand on the reins,
Went galloping out of control.

The poor boy's nose hit the chariot door,
He doubled over in pain,
Then a renegade star struck him square in the gut,
And his hands let go of the reins.

With no one in charge, the horses went wild.
Comets streamed from their manes.
Terrified, Phaëthon screamed at them, "STOP!"
But he could not remember their names.

When Phaëthon gazed from his dizzying height
To the antlike world of the ground,
His leg muscles twitched and his poor stomach heaved
At the thought of the long plummet down.

The chariot's crazy, zigzagging course
Took it way too close to the soil.
Thousands were killed as the mountaintops burned,
And the oceans started to boil.

The boy's skin blistered under the salve.
He tried in vain to draw breath,
But he gagged on the smoke that rose in plumes
From the earth that was burning to death.

On Olympus the deities watched with alarm
The chaos that raged in the skies.
Teardrops that smelled of barley and wheat
Fell from Demeter's eyes.

Great mother Gaia spoke to the gods,
Lifting her smoldering hands.
"Zeus, put an end to my suffering," she said,
"If you care at all for your lands."

"Forgive me, Apollo. Forgive me, my son,"
Said Zeus with a sorrowful voice,
"But my bolt shall be sharp and his death shall be quick;
I must make the obvious choice."

The bolt hit Phaëthon square in the chest,
Knocking him out of the car,
And as the boy's body fell to the earth,
He
   Lit
      Up
         The
            Sky
               Like
                  A
                     Star.

A beautiful Nereid discovered him there,
On the sands of a lonely isle.
Though charred by the lightning and scorched by the sun,
He still had Apollo's smile.

She set up a tomb on a high mountaintop
Where the sunset would kiss it with light,
And on the marble stone circled with laurel,
She had a great mason write . . .

Apollo put his hand on Iris's shoulder. He whispered,
"Shh, Amphitrite sings the coda." A spotlight came up on

the piano and Iris saw a woman lying there, smoking a cigarette in a long holder. Her skin was midnight blue, her hair sea green. She looked at Iris, winked, and blew a smoke ring in the shape of a fish. Iris felt a crazy urge to dive into the sea.

Amphitrite ended the story . . .

Nobody knows the trouble I've seen;
Nobody knows my blues.
Be careful what you wish for, kid;
Be careful what you choose.

I'm the one who buried the boy
Where the sun could kiss him good night.
I paid for the grave with the blue of my eyes,
    The smell of the ocean,
        The curve of my thighs,
            And a very fine bottle of octopus wine.
Here's what I told them to write:

Here lies Phaëthon, buried deep;
He tried to drive his father's jeep.
Mightily he tried;
Mightily he died.
Only two things soften sorrow:
Music, and
    Tomorrow.

Chapter 13

Iris sat on the edge of the stage and watched Amphitrite touch up her makeup. It was easy to see why she had stolen Poseidon's heart.

"I think you're very beautiful," Iris told her.

"I owe it all to my stylist." Amphitrite handed Iris a pink pearlized business card.

PAMPER YOURSELF LIKE A GODDESS AT
APHRODITE'S SWAN SALON
- *Hair, makeup, and wardrobe consultation*
- *For Very Special Women Only*
- *Located among the untrodden ways*
- *Open twenty-four hours, seven days*
- *For all your beauty emergencies*

"Thanks," Iris said. She put the card in her pocket. "But I'm not really that into makeup and stuff." Aphrodite was the goddess that interested Iris the least. She didn't really see how meeting her would help anything.

Amphitrite pulled the little seashells out of her hair, one by one. Soon it hung to her knees in sparkling waves of green. "Looking good never hurt anybody, kid. Besides, love is a powerful goddess. She must be honored."

"I guess you're right." Iris thought of Poseidon, wasting away for love. "Amphitrite, are you married?"

She smiled sadly. "I was, once. That was another lifetime."

"What happened?"

"All good things come to an end. In the beginning, it was all dolphin rides and octopus wine. But then his ardor waned. Gods are all the same, Iris: like a shallow well that dries up as soon as you get thirsty. Goddesses are different. *We run deeper.* Anyway, he was taking me for granted, and I can't stand that. So I left, to follow my dreams."

"Do you ever miss him?"

"Maybe a little, yeah. But it's water under the bridge. I put my suffering in my song. Do you know that, just tonight, seven ships crashed themselves while I did my little number?" Amphitrite looked at Iris with pride.

"Really? Because of your song?"

"Yep! Not bad, huh? Twenty sailors, dashed against the rocks. It happens every time I sing."

"But—don't you feel sad for them?"

"'Sad'?" Amphitrite looked at Iris with surprise. Her eyes were green and profound. Deep within them, little golden bubbles rose to the top and broke. There was something in her eyes that was fierce and frightening, beyond human emotions like pity. "They are one with the sea now. That is all."

Iris tried one more time. "But what if Po—your husband—was really sorry about how things were? What then?"

"Well, there's posters all over town. Why doesn't he come to a show and beg me to take him back?"

"But what if he's all alone and doesn't know how to find you? What if he's weak and dying because he's so sad?"

Amphitrite put her makeup away and patted Iris on the head. "You have a vivid imagination, kid." She left, and Iris sat on the stage, watching the drummer pack up his kit. She felt sort of empty and sad, like a radio that's been unplugged.

"It's called 'anticlimax,'" said Apollo. He sat down next to her on the stage and put his arm around her. He smelled like wonderful cologne. "It's when something cool happens and then when it's over, you feel let down. Musicians get anticlimax all the time. Onstage, life is fabulous. It's all hot lights and rhythm and applause. Then the set ends and all the pretty ladies leave, and real life seems hollow. Can't let it get you down, though, kid. That's what happened to a lot of the lesser gods: killed by anticlimax."

"But I feel so sad, Apollo. So many things are messed up

and I can't fix them. There's my mom's job, and then there's Poseidon, who might die, and then"—she swallowed, feeling a lump in her throat—"well, that was a really sad story about your son, and it makes me want to cry, and most of all I'm sad because it's late now and I have to go to school in the morning. I don't know what to do."

"Well, you can do what musicians always do. Loiter at the bar."

"Do you mean alcohol?" Iris asked, surprised. "But I'm not old enough to drink."

"Come with me, kiddo," Apollo replied, then laughed. "I want to introduce you to someone."

Apollo led Iris to one side of the club and sat her on a stool at the bar. The counter was made of tin; it shone under the dim lights. It had a nice thick edge made just to lean your elbows on.

"Hey, Bro; it's Iris," Apollo yelled, and he left her there.

An extraordinary man appeared from behind the bar. His face bristled with piercings in unusual places. He had thick black ringlets, pale skin, and kohl-lined eyes like an Egyptian statue. He cried out with joy when he saw her. "Iris! Most fabulous! Dionysus at your service, duckling."

He bowed with a flourish. The piercings jingled. As he straightened back up, Iris saw with surprise that he was wearing a dress.

"Not a dress, Iris, a toga. I prefer to keep to the old fashions. This is real Tyrian purple. And look at the grape-leaf embroidery along the edge—isn't it darling? Athena made it for me for my birthday."

"You can read my mind, too, just like Apollo."

"It's a bartender's job to read the minds of his customers: to appear at the perfect moment, out of thin air, to refill their drinks; to be there when they need someone to talk to, and to disappear when they need to be alone. A bartender must be a master mind-reader. For example, right now"—he pressed his fingers to his temples and seemed to be concentrating very hard—"you are thinking how fabulous I am."

"Umm, well . . ."

He grinned. "Oh, sorry, that was what *I* was thinking."

When Dionysus talked, his hands came alive with gestures. He fanned out each long, ringed finger on its own as if trying to make bird shadows on the wall. He made Iris want to sit at the bar for hours.

"Dionysus, how did you and Apollo know I was coming? Did the woman who sent me these gifts call you, like she did Poseidon? Can you tell me who it is?"

He shook his head. "We found out from the Sibyl."

"The Sibyl? Who's that?"

"This homeless lady who lives in the basement. Apollo's the only one who can understand what she's saying. She comes out with a good prediction once in a while, though. She's especially good with the horse races."

"Could we ask her for a prediction about me, Dionysus?"

"Well, if you want to, kiddo, but I'm telling you, she's a few vines short of a vineyard." Dionysus lifted up a trapdoor behind the bar and yelled into it, "SIBYL! We need a prophecy for Iris."

An old woman's voice screeched out from below, "Hey-shortyit'syourbirthdayoopsIdiditagainIplayedmydrumfor-HimparumpupumpumIlikemybeatsfunkyI'mspunkyIlike-myoatmeallumpyI'vetraveledeachandeveryhighwaybut-muchmorethanthat,Ididitmyway!"

Dionysus copied it all down on a piece of paper. "See what I mean?" he said to Iris, and he waved Apollo over.

Apollo looked at the paper, then said, "If you go to war, a great empire will fall. Lucky numbers: twelve, ninety-two, and two hundred sixteen."

Iris thanked Apollo, although the prophecy made no sense to her. "But why would I go to war?"

"Don't ask me, kid," Apollo said, "I'm all about peace." And he went back to his table, where a last few guests were clustered. Dionysus produced a dusty wine bottle from behind the bar.

"So, little lady," he said, "drinks are on the house for all members of Apollo's band."

"You want me to drink wine? I'm only twelve, you know. You could get arrested."

He leaned over the bar to examine her. "Twelve, huh? I was hoping you were just extremely short for your age. You're sure you're not twenty-one? Just got the digits mixed up?"

Iris shook her head. "I just turned twelve."

He sighed. "I suppose that *is* a bit young. Zeus might get mad at me if he heard I was corrupting the youth. Still, perhaps just a sip? *I* started drinking when I was *three,* and look how great I've turned out! And as for getting arrested, I wouldn't worry about it. Ares is our lawyer, and he could get any charges dropped. Probably even counter-sue and get us extra money."

"Ares, the god of war?"

"Yep, he's gone into the law. Says it's pretty much the same thing as war."

"Oh." She wondered briefly if the Sibyl's prophecy could mean that she should go to court. "Did you say that you started drinking when you were *three,* Dionysus? Your parents let you do that?"

"Well, my parents weren't really around. My mother exploded when I was still a fetus."

"She exploded?" Iris didn't know what to say. He didn't seem to be joking. "I . . . I'm very sorry to hear that."

"It's okay. She kind of had it coming. Zeus was my father, and she asked him for a favor. He swore he would give her whatever favor she asked."

"Oh, no. Did he swear on the river Styx? That always seems to mean trouble."

"Sadly, he did. My mother, Semele, who was a mortal woman, asked him to appear to her in his full, immortal glory, the way he does on Mount Olympus. Hera put the idea in my mother's head, as a way to get rid of her. Hera's always jealous of Dad's girlfriends. Dad couldn't get Semele to change her mind, so he did what she asked. He put on what we call his 'lesser panoply.' That's sort of like your second-best party dress: not bad, but not the best you can do, either. Still, even the lesser panoply was too much for Mom's weak mortal frame. She exploded in the divine radiance."

He threw back his head and let out a peal of weeping. "Oh, sorrow! Oh, lamentation! Mommy!" He dropped to the ground as though he had been punched in the stomach, so that Iris had to lean over the bar to see him. He was writhing on the floor of the bar, gnashing his teeth, and letting out a strange keening sound. He kicked over a box, and peanuts flew everywhere. Just as Iris was wondering if she should call Apollo for help, Dionysus popped up, suddenly back to normal. He withdrew a purple sequin handkerchief from a fold in his toga and dabbed at his eyes. "It's okay," he said. "I'm a very emotional person." Iris found it a bit dizzying.

"Old wounds are the deepest. Even with thousands of years to get over it, it still makes me cry. Fortunately, Zeus saved me from Mother's womb and sewed me up in his thigh, where I grew up until I was ready to be born. Then he shipped me off to some nymphs, to raise me. So, the point of the story is, my parents did not care what I was doing at three, because one of them had exploded and the other was in heaven throwing thunderbolts. And even if they *had* been there, I doubt that they would have tried to stop me from drinking wine, since I was, after all, the one who invented it!"

"You invented wine?"

"Yes, ma'am."

Iris didn't tell Dionysus this, but she had tried wine once before, during a rare visit to her father's house, when she was six. It was Passover and they gave her a little plastic cup full of the stuff. She tried to drink it, but it tasted like grape juice that had gone funny. She slipped it under the table to the dog Dreidel, who got so drunk he spent the rest of the night spinning around in circles until he fell down. The whole experience had convinced her that wine was something to be avoided. Yet Dionysus looked so proud as he showed her the dusty bottle.

"This, my dear duckling, is a 1929 Haut-Brion. Ah, Paris in the twenties! I had the most fashionable wineshop in the city. Every weekend I would fill the store with grapes, knee-deep!" While he spoke, he wiped the bottle off with a white cloth and opened it with a corkscrew. When the cork came out, Iris swore she saw a tendril of smoke rise.

"I want you to pay attention now, Iris, because this is one of the very best wines from one of the very best vintages in history. What I mean is, if you don't like *this* wine . . . well, I'm afraid that you'll never amount to much."

Iris wasn't sure she agreed with that, and he looked up at her, cocking an eyebrow.

"Ah, so she disagrees, does she? Well, I'm afraid you're out of your depth here, Iris. *In vino veritas.* In wine, truth." He set a glass decanter on the bar and slowly poured the wine into it, using a candle behind the bottle to watch the way the wine poured out. Then he set the bottle aside and poured the wine from the decanter into two crystal glasses. The liquid shone a red brown in the dim light.

Iris decided she *would* take a sip, just one. When in Rome you were supposed to do what the Romans did, and she was in a jazz club. Plus, she was afraid if she said no, Dionysus might cry again.

He handed her one of the full wineglasses. "Hold it by the stem, so your hand doesn't heat up the wine." The glass was iridescent and soap-bubble-thin. Iris worried that she might drop it. "Yes, Iris, these are priceless crystal glasses from turn-of-the-century Vienna. And you can smash as many as you want! There is no point in owning beautiful things unless you are prepared to break them." He took an empty glass off the bar and tossed it over his shoulder. It smashed into the cash register and exploded into hundreds of pieces.

"Now, slowly, we approach the tasting. Wine is like a beautiful woman. Look at her first. Notice the color of her robe. Then, get close enough to smell her perfume." He showed Iris how to swirl the glass around. "You are lucky, Iris. You have a big nose. Put your whole nose in the glass and smell."

Iris inhaled. It was overwhelming.

"Yes," she said. "I smell flowers."

"What kind?"

"Violets."

"What else?" he asked.

"Cigarettes, burning leaves, and cough drops."

Dionysus touched his glass to hers, and a sweet crystal ringing filled the bar. She looked into his eyes and smiled. She knew how to do this. Her father had taught her.

"L'chaim," Iris said.

Dionysus laughed. "Excellent, child! *À la vie!* To life!" She took a little sip of the wine, then almost fell off her stool as the vision hit her. She was in the kitchen of a grand island villa. The windows were open wide; outside she saw sunshine and rocky beaches. A vase of violets and an earthenware jar filled with cookies sat in the center of a table. Iris watched as a beautiful young woman with tearstained cheeks crept into the room, looked around, and reached into the jar.

"Congratulations, Iris. You've got taste." Dionysus put his hand on Iris's shoulder to steady her as she put down the glass.

"Dionysus, that was delicious. Who was the girl?"

"Well, Iris, that was my wife, a long, long time ago. She's a constellation now." He poured himself the rest of the bottle, then began the story.

Chapter 14

I married my wife so she would stop crying. What else could I do? I was getting home from a fabulous party in Athens that had lasted all week, so I was absolutely exhausted. And there she was, camped out in my kitchen, eating cookies and crying. I don't know how she even got into the house.

When I cleared my throat she said, "Yes, can I help you?"

"No! I mean, yes." I was stunned. "I mean, it's MY house, after all! What are you doing here?"

"I am eating cookies and crying."

"Well, I can see that." There followed an awkward silence. Well, to me it felt awkward. Ariadne seemed totally comfortable. In fact, she put her feet up on the table.

"Well, don't just stand there," she said, "bring me some milk." She sniffled and wiped her eyes on my tablecloth. Then

she threw her arms to the sky and wailed, "Theseus, Theseus, why have you abandoned me?"

I don't know why I brought her the milk. Had I gotten some sleep the previous night, instead of drinking a bathtub full of brandy, I would have had the strength to do what any sane man would have done and thrown her out. But instead, I brought her milk, and that was the point of no return. After the milk, marrying her just seemed to follow logically. Thank Zeus she was mortal, because marriage to her was no fun at all. You see, I was just a consolation prize for Ariadne; she never stopped loving Theseus.

My wife first met Theseus when he came to her city to be fed to the Minotaur. Ariadne's father was the powerful King Minos of Crete. Crete had defeated Athens in a war, and the conditions of the peace treaty were horrible. Every year, Athens was required to send Crete seven youths and seven maidens. These poor young Athenians would be thrown to the Minotaur, a half-bull, half-human monster kept by King Minos in a great stone maze called a labyrinth. It was a terrible price to pay for peace.

King Minos used to let his daughter adopt one of the Athenian girls who were sent there to die. When the new crop came in, they would be lined up in front of the princess and she would select the maiden who struck her fancy.

"You will be my special pet," Ariadne would coo at her chosen one. That one would be led off to Ariadne's suite. The rest of the maidens and all of the youths were sent to holding cells in the dungeon while the priests began the monthlong preparations for the Sacrifice of the Fourteen.

Ariadne loved playing with her pet Athenian girls. It was the one time she was not bored, for the life of a rich princess in those days was quite dull. There was nothing to do except embroider, take naps, and wait for your father to find you a husband. Dreadful, really. So Ariadne passed the time by dressing up her pets in silly outfits, dyeing their hair with Tyrian purple, and giving them horrible makeovers that involved charcoal and sheep's dung. It was just like having a live doll.

The Athenian girls were terrified of the fate awaiting them in the labyrinth. So, even though they hated Ariadne and the way she treated them, they did not complain. They thought she meant to save them from the monster.

But they did not understand Ariadne. The first year that her father, against his better judgment, had allowed her to select a special friend from among the Athenian delegation, Ariadne was nine. The girl she selected, Delia, was fourteen and the daughter of a senator. The two girls became inseparable. For the first time in her life, Ariadne had a friend.

Delia had ambitions to be the first great woman mathematician. She took Ariadne out in the moonlight, to measure the lengths of their shadows, and showed how you could use that to calculate the size of the earth itself. She taught Ariadne beautiful words like lemma *and* axiom, congruency *and* isosceles.

Ariadne started telling everyone that she wanted to be a geometer, and that she and her friend Delia were going to open the first-ever women's mathematical academy and pastry parlor. It would teach girls about math and also serve delicious tarts, she explained. The adults smiled indulgently, but her father scowled. He knew there was a bad scene approaching.

"Delia belongs to the Minotaur, not to you," King Minos would warn. But Ariadne pretended not to hear him. In her heart, she felt sure that her father would give in at the last moment. He had always given in, her whole childhood. Whenever anyone would try to warn Minos about spoiling his daughter, he said he didn't care. "She has had enough pain, losing her mother at such a young age. Besides, I am very busy, and saying yes is easier."

Ariadne assured Delia, "My father always listens to me. He will never send you off. It is sad, yes, that the other girls have to die, but we will still have each other."

"Such a sweet child," Delia would say, looking into Ariadne's bright brown eyes, and would silently add, How can she be the child of such a tyrant? As the weeks passed, Delia allowed herself to forget the terror of the approaching sacrifice.

But one day, Ariadne's nurse came running into the girls' suite.

"Princess, Princess, your father is calling for the Athenian girl! He says the priests read in the entrails of a great eagle that today is an auspicious day to offer the fourteen. They are sending the Athenians right now to the temple to be dressed in white. He said to hurry and send him your girl to join the others."

"Tell him to make do without her. Tell him I will not give her up."

"But, Your Highness, he will not listen. He told me to bring her kicking and screaming if I must. He said the sacrifice cannot go on without her."

"Then, tell him you could not find us."

"Ariadne, he will kill me!"

"I do not care. I am not letting them take her. She is mine."

"Stubborn girl. Things would be different if your mother had lived. You would not have been left to grow up like a wild animal."

"I suggest you keep your advice to yourself, servant," snapped Ariadne. "My father will not kill her once he sees how much she means to me."

"Ha! There are some sides of your father you do not know about. When it comes to the Minotaur, your father will do whatever it takes to keep things quiet. He would sacrifice you if he thought he had to." The nurse stormed out, leaving Ariadne alone with Delia, who was sitting very still, her face pale.

"Delia, we must hide."

But Delia did not answer. Ariadne took her by the shoulders and looked into her eyes.

"Delia, are you okay?"

"Ariadne, I am going to die."

"No, you won't. That stupid nurse doesn't know what she's talking about. You'll see. My father is a very kind man. He won't let you die." Delia smiled.

"Ariadne, do you know what we call your father in Athens?"

"No."

"The Butcher of Crete. Your father has killed young people from my city for as long as I can remember. When I did something wrong, my old nurse used to tell me that the Butcher of Crete would come and get me and he would put me in the maze with his monster."

"But he won't kill you, Delia; you're different."

"How am I different, Ariadne?"

"You're my friend."

"Oh, so your friend doesn't deserve to die, but all the other girls and boys do?" Delia's voice was harsh.

"Oh, Delia, let's not fight. Please. Let's go hide. Father will be on his way here any second."

Delia sat up very straight. "I am the daughter of a senator of Athens. I will not hide like a coward, but will look death in the eye."

"But, Delia, you're not going to die. My father won't—"

"Your father! The Butcher!" Delia sounded mean now. "He told the nurse to bring me kicking and screaming."

"But, Delia . . ." Ariadne began to cry. She held her arms out to her friend.

Delia, dry-eyed, laughed. "Poor Ariadne! Do you ever think of anyone but yourself? Did it ever bother you before that your father killed fourteen children a year? No, it only bothers you now that it involves your little pet.

"Well, how do you think I feel? I'm the one being sent to die! I'm the one who gets dressed in white and led into the maze, while you sit with the royal ladies in the pavilion." Delia shivered. "Don't you think I want to cry? Don't you think I feel ashamed that I let myself hope? That I slept on satin sheets while the others were in a dungeon? That I made friends with the daughter of my executioner? I should have spit in your face the moment I met you. Well, I'll make up for lost time."

King Minos walked in just as the spit hit his daughter's face.

"You see what happens when you make friends with them?"

he said as his guards threw Delia to the floor and bound her with chains.

Ariadne wiped the spit and tears from her face and looked at her father. He smiled at her and smoothed the hair back from her forehead. He had not done that to her since she was a little girl. "My little Ari, don't be sad. This one will scream as she dies. And then, next year, you can have another pet from the new crop. But you won't get so close next time, hmm?"

Ariadne looked down at Delia, who was struggling like a wild animal, then looked away quickly.

"Father, may I have cakes to eat today as we watch the sacrifice?"

"Of course, my pet."

"And may I wear Mother's diamond-and-emerald necklace?"

"I shall have the slaves bring it right away." The guards lifted Delia up. Although small, she was bucking and writhing with such force that it took three strong men to carry her out. The captain of the guard, Scipio, was talking to her in soothing undertones.

"There, there, little tiger. We don't want to hurt the princess's friend. Relax, now."

"And, Scipio?" barked Ariadne.

"Yes, Your Highness!" Scipio saluted.

"No need to give this one any special treatment. She is nothing to me."

"Yes, Your Highness." They carried Delia out, and Ariadne was left alone with her father.

"You will make quite a queen someday, my girl," he said.

"A master of your emotions, just like your father." Suddenly, Ariadne wished very much that he would hold her, but she could not remember him ever having done so. She walked up to her father and hugged him. Minos stiffened, thumped her back three times, and peeled her off.

"Well, then," he said. "I'll, uh, have that necklace sent to you right away." And he walked out, leaving her alone.

After Delia, Ariadne never again made the mistake of seeing the doomed maidens as people. They were like toys to her, and she grew quite good at giving them up. When the time came, she would say to her father, "Oh good, Papa. I was growing so tired of this one!"

This all changed the summer of Ariadne's fifteenth year. Her father should perhaps have seen it coming, but like many adults, he forgot what it was to be a teenager. That summer, when the seven youths and seven maidens were lined up in front of the king, Ariadne could not take her eyes off Theseus.

King Aegeus of Athens was a desperate man. His people were sick with grief from sending fourteen children a year to die in Crete. Theseus was King Aegeus's brave, arrogant son, a virtuoso with the sword, who had already killed many monsters on the roads surrounding Athens. This was his chance to shine. Theseus had promised his father that he would slay the Minotaur and return the thirteen others safely home. Amid great mourning, the fourteen children had set off for Ariadne's city, in a ship with black sails. If the children died, the crew would sail back with the same black sails flying. But if he won,

Theseus promised his father Aegeus that he would hoist white sails to bring them all home.

Ariadne stared and stared at the hero who stood in her father's throne room. He was a full head taller than the other youths. His eyes shone with arrogance. His chest puffed out like a rooster. He looked as relaxed as if he were in his own castle.

"I want this one, Father," said Ariadne, standing in front of Theseus. Theseus eyed her with amusement.

"But, Ariadne dear, he's . . . well, we never discussed—"

"I know that I usually select one of the girls, but they are utterly useless." Ariadne managed to sound cool, though her little heart was pounding in her chest. "You know that I have that addition I've been wanting to make to the solarium. This one can help me carry the marble."

"We have plenty of slaves for that, Ariadne."

"But I also want to learn archery. And Scipio is an awful teacher. He can't even shoot straight himself." Turning to Theseus, she said, "Boy, are you skilled at archery?"

Theseus murmured so that only Ariadne and the Athenian boy next to him could hear, "You are already pierced, it seems, and I did not even aim." The other boy sniggered; Ariadne blushed.

Theseus cleared his throat and said aloud, "Princess, I am the finest archer in Athens. From a hundred paces, I can shoot a butterfly in flight. From five hundred paces I can shoot the petals off a daisy, one by one. I can shoot the wool off a sheep and leave him perfectly sheared. I can shoot the filling out of a spanakopita and leave the phyllo intact. I can shoot the sorrow out of a widow and the love of money out of a gambler. And *it would be my honor"—he bowed low—"to teach the lovely Princess Ariadne."*

Ariadne, who had listened to his speech openmouthed, turned to her father and said, "See, Papa?"

If her father were in the habit of paying attention to his daughter, he would have noticed the transformation in Ariadne: the nervous agitation in her voice, the flush in her cheeks, the bright gleam in her eyes.

But he had spent his whole life ignoring things like that.

"Yes, fine, I suppose there's no harm in it. Just remember, he dies in the end, just like all the rest."

"I know, Papa," said Ariadne, enraptured.

Theseus took advantage of his position as the princess's companion to use every spare moment preparing for his battle with the Minotaur. Ariadne trotted along at his heels like a puppy. Though she loved to see him practice, the thought of him battling a real-life foe filled her with fear, and she tried to convince him to abandon his quest and make off with her.

"Fine," said Ariadne one day. "If you insist on endangering your life, I can't stop you. But I won't send you in there empty-handed. Here." She laid King Aegeus's sword before him. The sword had been seized when Theseus first arrived, but Ariadne had bribed the guards into giving it back to her.

"Fabulous," said Theseus, holding the sword up so it caught the light. He swung it back and forth through the air. Ariadne sat down to watch him, her elbows on her knees. The sword made a singing sound as it sliced the air in two.

"You're so cool, Theseus. Do you promise, once you've killed the Minotaur, to take me far away from here?"

"I promise to take you far away from here, Princess."

"And do you promise to love me? Will you repay my sacrifices?"

"I promise," he said, setting the sword down, "to give you all the gratitude you deserve."

Dionysus put a hand on Iris's shoulder. "If you feel a funny feeling in your stomach," he said, "don't worry. It's just irony. Maybe you think Ariadne is silly for not noticing all this irony. But you must remember that love blurs the mind, worse than wine. That is why we have to be very careful when we drink wine, and very, very careful when we fall in love. There is a warning label on whiskey bottles that says DRINK RESPONSIBLY. But there is no warning label on people that says WARNING: SHE WILL THROW MILK SHAKES WHEN PROVOKED. Or DANGER: HE IS JUST USING YOU FOR YOUR ALGEBRA NOTES. In love, Iris, we are on our own."

Ariadne asked Theseus how he planned to find his way out after killing the Minotaur.

"What do you mean? I'll just retrace my steps."

Ariadne laughed. "Theseus, don't you know anything? No one can retrace their steps in the labyrinth. It's a giant maze the size of an amphitheater. What you need is a way to retrace your path. I know!" She ran to a trunk in her bedroom and came back holding something shiny.

"What is it?" asked Theseus.

"It's yarn. It's very rare, made from the Golden Fleece. They say that only two such skeins were ever made. One was given

to the goddess Athena. The other was given to my great-great-grandmother as a wedding gift. It has been passed down through the women in my family. It shines in the dark like soft sunlight."

"What do I do with it?"

"Tie it to something near the entrance. Then unwind it behind you as you go through the maze. It has magic in it, this yarn. It will be as long as you need it to be. When you get done killing the Minotaur"—Ariadne shivered—"just follow the yarn back. I will unlock the gates and have your ship waiting at the docks."

"Thank you, Ariadne." He kissed her, and she glowed, brighter than the yarn.

The day for the sacrifice came, and Ariadne tearfully sent Theseus off. In addition to the sword and yarn, she had found him a thin breastplate to wear under his clothes. She sat in the stands and wept, long after all the crowds had left, and stared at the locked gates to the labyrinth. When the gates swung shut behind him, Theseus was glad for the light of the yarn. The silence was thick in the dark maze, and the air smelled like a campfire. There were Athenian bones everywhere. Theseus addressed his companions: "I think we will see many terrible sights in the labyrinth, and we will need to stick together. And keep quiet."

They obeyed, and they soon found that Theseus was right. They did see terrible things in the labyrinth: piles of bones, scenes of desperate combat, messages written in blood. The group began to feel as if they were in some sort of horrible theater.

The great director behind this production was the Minotaur. It took the Minotaur about four hours to kill the typical group of fourteen children, but he soon got bored with that. He began to stretch it out, to prolong the pleasure of the hunt, leaving his victims water and little snacks of roasted rats.

Like most monsters, the Minotaur was not such a bad guy. He had tried to make friends with the first few bunches of victims. But of course, they ran and screamed when they saw him. He was hideous: muscular, hunchbacked, and covered with red-brown fur. Horns curved from his forehead, and his eyes glowed a fearsome red.

The Minotaur was Ariadne's half brother, born in shame to Minos's wife. The queen had been pricked by one of Eros's arrows and, unfortunately, the first thing she looked at was a tall, dark, handsome bull. What should have been the best day of King Minos's life—the day his wife bore a son—was the worst. The boy looked nothing like Minos and everything like the bull. The queen died in childbirth. The midwife was killed. The great architect Daedalus was sent for, to build a prison in which to hide the child.

Minos was terrified that someone would find out about his wife's sin, so he told everyone the baby had been born dead. He invented a story about a terrible monster, called "the Minotaur," that had been sent down by the gods, and he forbade anyone to go near the labyrinth where the beast was imprisoned.

Minos assumed that the child was an idiot, since he did not speak but simply grunted and snorted. Minos was, however, wrong. The Minotaur was highly intelligent and was born un-

derstanding everything that was said around him. The only thing he did not understand was why people were so unkind to him and acted so scared. He was just a child. He did not understand shame.

I have always wished that Ariadne could have learned the truth about the Minotaur earlier. My wife had many faults, but I know that if she had known the creature was her half brother, she would have gone to him. Her natural stubbornness would have led her to him, and perhaps the two could have been friends. For they had more in common than you would think. The Minotaur lived alone in his dark stone maze; Ariadne lived alone in a maze of empty shiny things. But by the time Theseus got to him, it was too late for kindness. The Minotaur had become a monster.

Theseus need not have worried about the group's keeping their voices down. The Minotaur knew the moment they entered the labyrinth. Just as the spider knows with intimate precision which strands the fly has touched, so the Minotaur felt the tension in his maze as the children traveled through it. But something was different about this group of children. They did not scream when they saw the Wall of Ears. No one had killed themselves. And, what was worse, they were messing with the displays. They were taking all the skulls and carrying them around, to take back to Athens for burial. It made him very angry. He decided to finish this group off quickly, before they could mess up his eyeball mosaic. Leaving the roasted rats in his lair, he galloped with terrible speed down the corridors, following the scent of children. The battle rage came upon him and he smiled a horrible smile. He was hungry.

"When we face the Minotaur, I will take him. Alone," said Theseus. "If I fail, you will all have your turns to try, but I want the first shot. We will meet him here, by the torches, where I can see him better." Theseus was trembling with excitement. He sensed the Minotaur's approach. He put his ear to the floor. "Yes, I hear him coming."

The other children clustered together behind a mound of fingers. Theseus drew his sword. The wait was awful. For a while, all was silent, except for the sputtering of the torches and the quickened beating of their hearts. But then a rumbling approached. It grew louder and became mixed with snorting and snuffling sounds—the sounds of an angry animal.

Then he was upon them. Straightening up onto his hind legs, the Minotaur towered over Theseus, immensely strong, the strongest foe Theseus had ever faced. Smoke came out of the beast's nostrils and he stared at the boy with open hatred.

Theseus met the glowing red eyes and drew in a deep breath. "His will is strong," he whispered. "This will be hard." Theseus was filled with joy, for he loved battle above all else. He threw back his head and laughed.

The Minotaur leveled his horns and charged. He caught Theseus in the chest, and knocked him down onto his back. Theseus's sword spun away into a corner, and if it hadn't been for Ariadne's breastplate, he might have been killed. The Minotaur leaped onto the fallen boy, pinning him against the rocky floor. Theseus was caught in a bad position: When he covered his face, he left his ribs open to bruising punches. When he covered his ribs, he got punched in the face. Through puffy lips he said, "You punch like a girl. And you're ugly."

The Minotaur roared and punched harder. Theseus's left eye had swollen shut, but still he waited for his opening, taunting the Minotaur in between blows. "Your mother must have been the ugliest cow in the herd."

That did it. The Minotaur didn't remember anything about his mother, but Theseus's words hit the empty place where she should have been. The beast lifted his head to the ceiling and bellowed so fearfully that the listening children clapped their hands to their ears. Theseus punched the Minotaur hard in the face and bucked his hips. The Minotaur was thrown backward.

Both leaped to their feet. For a moment they stared at each other, breathing hard. The blood flowing from Theseus's nose made little red sunbursts on the floor. That last punch had broken Theseus's hand. He held it limp against his chest and eyed his sword, just out of reach.

The Minotaur shook his head to clear it, then smiled at the boy's predicament. It was time for the deathblow. He aimed his horns at the boy's neck this time. Theseus saw it coming but was powerless to react.

Just then, the smallest and weakest boy, Davus, ran out from behind the fingers and threw himself on his belly, in the beast's path. The Minotaur hit Davus at full speed and went flying. Davus looked up, shocked at his success. The Minotaur had fallen a few inches from Theseus's feet. By this time, Theseus had his sword. He held it in his good, left hand and prodded the Minotaur in the shoulder.

"Get up and fight. We're not done yet."

The Minotaur shot out a hand and grabbed the sword by the blade. Theseus tried to pull it away, but the Minotaur would not let go, though blood oozed out between his fingers. Theseus shook the sword side to side. The blade cut deeper, but still the Minotaur would not let go. The two foes stared at each other.

"You are very brave," said Theseus, "but you must know your place. I am the hero and you are the monster." The Minotaur's breath came in rapid shallow snorts. "This was my father's sword." Theseus gritted his teeth and dug his heels into the ground. "He gave it to me."

The two kept pulling. Both of them were covered in the Minotaur's blood. Theseus spoke again, with difficulty. "Your father gave you nothing. Not even a name." The Minotaur let go and hung his head.

"Pity is a weakness," said Theseus as he struck deeply to the heart. The stroke was awkward, left-handed, but it was enough. When the Minotaur's body shuddered out its last breath, the stones wept. A great sigh ran through the empty corridors. And then the labyrinth itself began to die.

"Hurry," Theseus yelled as stones began to rain down from the walls. He wiped his sword off on the Minotaur's furry thigh. Rocks were falling from everywhere. A fist-sized stone struck one girl on the temple, and she tumbled to the ground. Theseus scooped her up over one shoulder and began to run, following the golden yarn. The rest followed.

Davus stopped halfway and sank down on his knees. He wrapped his arms around his stomach.

"I—," he wheezed, "I can't."

Theseus did not argue, but bent down and scooped Davus up over his other shoulder, wincing at the pain in his right hand. Doubled over by the weight, he ran even faster than be-

fore. Stones fell until the night sky shone through the maze's ceiling. Artemis looked down from her silver chariot and saw them. She shot silver arrows to clear their path.

Ariadne was waiting by the unlocked gates. When Theseus came out with Davus over his right shoulder and the maiden over his left, Ariadne ran to him, cooing.

"Oh, you're soooo brave. Oh, no! What happened to your hand?" Theseus's hand had swollen and discolored. He was covered with blood, his own and the Minotaur's. All the Athenians were bruised and coated in dust. Ariadne, however, shone softly in the moonlight, immaculate in golden silk. Even her toenails were painted with gold leaf.

"What happened to my yarn?" she said, pouting.

Theseus said, "Oh, I'm so sorry. What with killing the Minotaur and saving my friends from the avalanche, I somehow forgot to bring it back with me. Perhaps you'd like me to go back in there and get it? I mean, I could probably manage to dodge the flying boulders long enough to wrap it up neatly for you."

Ariadne sighed, then said she supposed she would do without it. She led them to the ship.

And you know the rest of the story, Iris. Theseus told them to dock on Naxos so he could take advantage of the famous hunting. He told Ariadne, secretly, that the real reason was so he could spend some time alone with her.

"Oh, the boat, it's so crowded," he said. "Let's go off into the woods all by ourselves so we can have some privacy."

Once they were alone, he gave her some drugged wine and left her asleep on a bank of moss. Chivalry is dead! She could have been devoured by wild beasts. His ship sailed off. But bad deeds have a way of coming back to the doer. In his haste to be rid of Ariadne and set sail for home, Theseus had forgotten one thing: the color of the sails. They were still the same mournful black as when he set off for Crete.

When Theseus gazed with joy at the first hints of Athens, his father gazed back from the top tower of his castle. King Aegeus shaded his eyes with his hand as he saw the tiny ship on the horizon. He had gone up to the turret every morning for a month, searching the ocean for his son. The king's heart beat faster. He had a feeling that this was the ship. But were the sails black or white? At this distance it was impossible to see. He waited.

Long after the sails' color was clear, Aegeus continued to wait. Perhaps it is just a trick of the light, *he thought,* just a shadow on the sea. *He waited. He felt sick. He thought of how young and brave his son had been.* Theseus was so sure he would win, *the king thought,* that he clouded my judgment. Oh how foolish I was! I believed that a slip of a boy could beat the Minotaur! Why did I let him go? Why did I let my son go to his death?

Aegeus threw himself off the tower and into the sea. And so, instead of a victory march, a funeral dirge greeted Theseus as he strode into the city. When he learned of his father's death, Theseus tore at his clothes with grief. The sails! How he wished he could go back in time and change the sails! But it was too late.

Chapter 15

"And speaking of too late"—Dionysus looked at his watch—"it's past one A.M. That was a long story. How are you holding up, plum blossom?"

"I'm great!" said Iris, but she couldn't suppress a yawn. "That was a super story, Dionysus."

"Excellent. Come back when you're twenty-one and I'll tell you lots more. Now, go wait with Atlas and we'll make sure you get home okay. I'm just going to close out the register."

Iris found Atlas standing by the door with Apollo, counting money. He handed a big wad of bills to Apollo, and Apollo slipped it into a gold money-clip.

"Did you make a lot of money tonight, Apollo?" Iris asked.

He laughed. "No one ever went into jazz for the money, baby." He peeled a few bills off the roll and handed them to her. "Here. I wish we could afford more."

Iris looked at the money. It was sixty whole dollars! "What is this for, Apollo?"

"For the gig. We pay sixty a set."

Iris couldn't believe it. He was paying her for singing! "But, Apollo, I couldn't've sung if you hadn't—"

"Shh, kid," said Atlas. "Never argue with a paycheck. And, you know, if you want to make a bit more, I'd be willing to take those old LPs off your hands for another thirty dollars."

"Wow, Atlas, that would be great."

But just as Iris reached out for the money, a stentorian voice cut through the room. "Iris, don't touch that cash!"

She snatched her hand back guiltily. An old man wheeled over to them and put his arm around her. He had a hawkish face, with a spear-shaped scar down one cheek. His wheelchair was covered with bumper stickers that said SEMPER FI.

"Ares," Atlas said, disappointed.

Ares saluted him. "Let me see those, Atlas, if you please." He grabbed the bag from Atlas and made a great show of going through each one, periodically exclaiming, "Oh, this is very rare!" and, "Ah! An import!" At the end he looked up at Atlas and said, "We won't take less than a C-note."

"*We?*" said Atlas.

"Yes, Iris is my client."

"Fine. I'll give you fifty," Atlas said.

Ares laughed. "The Brownie McGhee is autographed."

"Sixty."

"Atlas, you should be ashamed of yourself, taking advantage of a sleepy child and a handicapped veteran."

"Seventy."

"All right, but we keep the Coltrane."

"Eighty, *with* the Coltrane, and that's my final offer."

"How about ninety? It's for the child's education. Just look at her, poor thing. Her eyes, thirsty for knowledge."

Atlas growled. "Fine, eighty-five dollars, but only if you shut up now."

"Done. My lips are sealed."

Atlas counted out the money and gave it to Ares, who handed seventy dollars over to Iris, explaining that he took the rest as negotiator's fee. "It's a tough world, soldier; you've gotta make bread wherever you can."

"You're really good at that, Ares."

"Thanks, soldier. I love the law. It's even more fun than war."

Iris thought of the Sibyl's prophecy again. She had an idea. "Ares, have you ever sued a *company*?"

"Of course! That's the most fun of all, since companies have lots of money. The wise general only declares war on the rich."

Iris explained her mother's situation. "Do you think what Tofu-licious did is illegal, Ares? Firing my mom for a robot?"

Ares smiled. He took a wicked little knife from his pocket, spread his left hand on a table, and began to stab the knife up and down between his fingers. The knife moved so fast it was a blur. As Ares did this, he spoke: "You see, Iris, the question is not whether they broke the law or not. The question is who has the better lawyer. And I guarantee, *you* have the better lawyer. I don't mean to brag, Iris, but when the battle lust comes upon me, I am unstoppable."

"But Ares, I don't want to *hurt* anyone. I just want my mom to get her job back, or to get enough money so we can pay the rent."

"Listen, soldier, you leave it to me. Now, first things first: Know thy enemy. I've never gone up against Tofu-licious before. We'll need to get a sense of the lay of the land, the strength of the commander, the Achilles' heels." He reached into a pocket in the wheelchair and pulled out a cell phone and a Rolodex. "We've gotta bring in some finesse on this one, Iris." He dialed. "Ares here. You got time? . . . New client . . . Corporate espionage . . . Done." He hung up and wrote an address down on a slip of paper. "Go to this address tomorrow afternoon. I employ a private firm to do my reconnaissance. They're good, real good. You will explain to them the situation and they will begin the hunt." Then he saluted her. "Be of good courage, soldier! I'll see you at the next battle."

On her way out, Iris asked Apollo if he knew where to find any of the other gods. He said that the only one he stayed in touch with was his sister, who had gone into business with Athena. He gave Iris the address of their office. It wasn't until Iris got home and emptied out her pockets that she realized the addresses she had gotten from Apollo and Ares were the same. Athena and Artemis were private detectives.

Chapter 16

Iris lay in bed and listened to the sounds of her mother's snoring through the thin walls of the apartment. It was three in the morning, and Iris had never been awake this late before. She tried to make herself fall asleep, but it didn't work, not even with the dream quilt stretched over her head. Iris looked up at the golden words and smiled. It seemed as if she had written those out so long ago. Now her real life was even better than dreams.

She got up and tiptoed into the living room. Light from the parking lot crept through the spider plants to fall in jungle patterns on the floor. It was so quiet outside you could hear the faint humming of the electrical lines and the singing of the cicadas. Behind them, if you listened hard, you heard the rush of air as cars sped by on the turnpike.

Iris watched her mother sleep. There was only one bedroom in their apartment, and Helen had given it to Iris. Helen said she preferred the living-room couch, where she could be surrounded by her plants and their oxygen. Her mother looked very small beneath her quilt. If it weren't for the enormous snores, you wouldn't have even known she was there.

"Have sweet dreams, Mom," Iris whispered. "Everything's gonna be okay. The gods are on our side."

Iris opened the refrigerator and stared in dismay at the soy cheese and the aloe vera juice. She padded back to bed and tried to clear her mind. It was no use. Every time Iris closed her eyes, she heard saxophone music and saw Amphitrite's eyes. Or else she heard the sound of waves and saw Poseidon lying on the sand, weeping. She sat up and reached for the shiny pink card on her nightstand.

It smelled of roses. *Who ever heard of a hair salon open around the clock? And where were "the untrodden ways"?* Iris was suddenly seized with curiosity. *Well, since I can't sleep,* she reasoned, *I might as well go pay Aphrodite a visit.* That's loads better than sitting around in bed, waiting for the alarm to ring.

Iris spread the rainbow out on the floor.

"Πυρρός
Σανδαράκινος
Ξανθός
Χλωρός

ʿΥακίνθινος

Πορφύρεος

ʾΙοειδής"

The rainbow flowed up from the floor and out into the silent evening. Iris read the address aloud from the business card: "Aphrodite's Swan Salon, among the untrodden ways."

Dazzling sunlight filled her eyes. When her eyes adjusted, Iris saw that she stood in a clearing paved in white stone and surrounded on all sides by trees.

"Where *is* this place?" she murmured. "It must be on the other side of the *world,* it's so bright here."

A small bench carved from pink wood sat in the center of the clearing, with a rose vine twined around it. Iris wrapped the rainbow around her and sat down on the warm wood. The roses were fragrant. The sun seemed to fall extra thickly on the bench, and the leaves of the trees overhead quivered a lullaby. When Iris fell asleep, she dreamed that she was sitting in a warm rain shower that smelled like apricot and chamomile. It felt delicious. She let her head hang back over the edge of the bench, and she murmured in her sleep, "Aphrodite."

"No," said a soft voice. "I'm Psyche. I'm just the shampoo girl. Aphrodite will do your haircut."

Iris opened her eyes. Everything was pink and sparkly. Her clothes had been replaced by a pink silk robe. Her feet were soaking in a silver basin filled with champagne. The woman washing Iris's hair smiled. She had long silver hair, and a butterfly tattoo on one cheek.

"Where am I?"

"The Swan Salon: a complete, full-service beauty paradise, run by the goddess of love herself and her humble entourage." Psyche bowed, revealing large gauzy butterfly wings tied to her back with ribbons.

"How did I get here?"

"Through the lady's grace. It's a precaution. We don't let anyone come here directly or it would ruin the glamour. We're among the untrodden ways here, and no one can find us unless we want to be found. See?" Psyche opened the front door to the salon, revealing outside nothing but a white empty expanse, stretching as far as Iris could see.

The Swan Salon looked like it had been attacked by a giant can of pink paint. There were pink plush carpets, pink walls, a pink tiled ceiling, and pink marble columns. All along one side ran a row of fancy pink vinyl chairs facing a mirror. It didn't seem possible, but rosebushes grew up out of the carpet and twined around the chairs. On the opposite side of the room, there was a small heart-shaped pool filled with glitter and a bored-looking swan.

"Don't go near the swan," said Psyche. "He bites."

Suddenly harp music filled the air. A crystal chandelier descended from the ceiling. Doves appeared out of nowhere and flew across the room. The swan hissed.

"It's Aphrodite's entrance, Iris. Look impressed."

The glitter cascaded down Aphrodite's sides as she rose up from the heart-shaped pool on a huge scallop shell. It was just like in statues, except way more impressive. Iris felt like she could spend the rest of her life looking at

Aphrodite's face. With her olive skin and dark almond-shaped eyes, Aphrodite could have been from any place, from any age. She was beauty itself. Her hair was covered in glitter and hung to her waist in thick curls of blue black.

"Hey, snap out of it!" Psyche moved her hand in front of Iris's eyes.

Iris looked up, dazed.

"I said to look impressed, not hypnotized."

"It's just . . . she's so beautiful. I couldn't breathe."

"I know. She has that effect on people." Psyche smiled. "But look at her now."

Iris looked back. Aphrodite was trying to get out of the pool, but the swan had bitten her skirt and would not let go. She kicked the swan and yelled, "Adonis, you idiot, let go!" Glitter flew everywhere. Finally the skirt ripped off, and the swan swam off happily, chewing it.

Aphrodite climbed out of the pool in her pink lace underwear and threw her arms up. "That stupid swan!" She pulled a wand out of her sleeve and aimed it at her waist.

"Pretty as a picture,
Sharp as a tack,
Stonewashed denim,
A-line, black."

A black jean miniskirt wrapped itself around Aphrodite's hips. Psyche applauded and yelled, "Smashing!"

Aphrodite laughed and walked to Iris, her curtain of hair swaying from side to side. She took Iris's face between silky hands, which smelled of jasmine. Aphrodite's gaze was filled with love. Even her mother had never looked at Iris that way: with pure love, unmixed with any other emotion.

"Psyche," Aphrodite said, "get the color ready. Medium ash-blond and . . ." She let go of Iris's cheeks and fingered her hair. "Foxy Sunset. Iris, what I have in mind for you is some subtle highlighting. Nothing too aggressive, just some encouragement to your natural blond and red high tones."

Iris had no idea what Aphrodite was talking about. "But Aphrodite, I really just came here to meet you."

"I know just why you came, child. I know better than you know it yourself, in fact. You're on a journey, and you don't know the point of it yet. But you will. And then you will need keys to open doors. Beauty, Iris. Beauty opens doors."

"I'm sorry, Aphrodite, but I don't know what you mean."

"Don't worry, you'll figure it out. Now, where did I put the beauty? It's around here somewhere." Aphrodite reached into a cabinet beneath the mirror, rummaged around, and pulled out two boxes wrapped in silver foil and tied with pink ribbons. "Here. The little one's for Persephone and the bigger one's for Hera. They've both been too long without a visit here. These boxes have a little extra of my beauty in them, Iris. They'll sprinkle this on and look good as new, for a while at least."

"Wow, thanks." Iris took the boxes, which felt very light, as if there were nothing inside them. She held one up to her ear and shook it.

Aphrodite and Psyche laughed. "It's in there, Iris, I guarantee," said Aphrodite. "But woe unto you if you open it yourself. Do you understand? They must go directly to Hera and Persephone, no one else."

"Okay." It was true: Iris had been thinking that she might just slip the foil off, once she got outside, and take a little peek inside one of them. She was just curious.

"I mean it, Iris," said Aphrodite.

"But Aphrodite, I don't know how to find Persephone and Hera."

Aphrodite thought for a moment. "Well, I've lost track of Hera and Zeus. They're in the suburbs somewhere. Athena should know where. As for Persephone, she'll find you, sooner or later. Psyche, is the color ready?"

"Yes, Your Fabulosity."

"Well, first we have to take care of the horrible haircut. Iris, Iris, Iris." Aphrodite put her hand on Iris's shoulder and led her to one of the chairs. "What were you thinking when you went to this butcher? What did your hair ever do to you?"

Iris looked at her reflection in the mirror. Aphrodite had a point. "Well, the Hair Barn is only fifteen dollars a cut, Aphrodite. We need to save our money for more important things."

"Do you really think so?" Aphrodite sighed, then looked at her nails, which were long and perfectly shining. "I suppose that's why I'm the goddess of beauty and Athena is the goddess of wisdom. To me, nothing is more important than the right haircut."

She pointed her wand at Iris's head.

"Past the waist,
To the ankle.
Men will gape,
Women, rankle."

Iris's head snapped back, from the sudden weight of the long, luxurious hair that sprouted from her scalp. She shook her head from side to side and felt the heavy silken ripple.

"Wow, Aphrodite." Iris didn't know what to say. She ran her hands through her hair. It slid between her fingers without a single tangle. "But it might look a little suspicious if my hair grows this much overnight."

"Of course it would, Iris. Don't be silly. I intend to cut it to match your old length, but with a little more style. This is just the blank canvas upon which I will paint my masterpiece."

"Hello, lovely ladies!" The door opened with a jingling of chimes, and a man walked in from the emptiness. His head was covered with golden curls, and he carried a basket filled with pastry. "I'm just flying back from that darling bakery where we celebrated our one-thousandth anniversary, Psyche; do you remember it? Ah, Paris! Here, everyone, have some pastry."

He reached over his shoulder and grabbed a golden bow. In a flash, he set an arrow to the bow, put a croissant on the tip of the arrow, and shot it straight at Iris. She had no time to scream. The arrow thudded into the headrest of her chair, right next to her left ear. Crumbs fell onto her shoulder.

103

"Gosh, Eros! Be careful with that thing," said Psyche.

"I'm sorry," said the man, "but my aim is true, Psyche. You know that." He handed Iris a jar of cherry jam. Psyche kissed him.

"Iris, this is my husband, Eros. Sweetie, this is our little Iris."

"Iris!" Eros exclaimed. "Well, this *is* a treat. Seems like just yesterday I was shooting your father while he looked at your mother."

"Really? Wow. It always *did* seem weird to me that they fell in love," Iris said.

He shrugged. "I wouldn't really call it love."

"Eros!" Aphrodite scolded. "Behave yourself."

"Sorry, Mom." He pouted.

"But, Eros, why did you shoot my dad?"

"I was bored, and I was mad that all the gods moved to Pennsylvania and New Jersey. It was Zeus's idea. He thought we could fade in, live normal lives. But we aren't normal! I'm Eros, and I need to have my fun. And your mom seemed so serious. She needed a little excitement in her life. Besides, good came of it. You're here, aren't you?"

Iris munched on a croissant. "Well, I'm not sure you should play with people's lives like that." She thought of her father in Wisconsin, hunched over his Bible. "I mean, it doesn't seem respectful."

"I'm sorry, Iris." He didn't look at all sorry, though. "Hey, how 'bout I make it up to you by shooting someone for you? I guarantee whomever you love shall be yours. Whoever has run from you soon shall give chase! Whoever has scorned your gifts soon shall be the giver! Whoever has laughed at you soon shall weep with longing!"

"She's too young for that," said Psyche.

But Iris did have someone she wanted shot. She had not forgotten the weeping man on the seashore and her silent promise to help him. Eros stared into Iris's eyes and exclaimed, "Aha! She is young but precocious. Iris, I understand you perfectly. *Je te comprends.* Say no more! I am off on a mission of loooove. My arrows are sweet and swift. She won't know what hit her." With a jingle of chimes, he was gone.

The scent of ammonia filled the air as Aphrodite began painting strands of Iris's hair with creamy dye and wrapping them up in aluminum foil. Psyche handed Iris a cup of coffee with lots of cream and sugar, to go with the croissant. Iris did not like coffee, but she figured she'd better drink it, since she was staying up all night. To her surprise, it was delicious.

"Psyche, I need more foil strips," said Aphrodite.

But Psyche did not respond. She was looking at Iris's free hand, which was reaching out to stroke the silver boxes of beauty. Iris pulled her hand back, guiltily. She hadn't even realized she was doing that. It was as if the boxes were magnets, pulling her to them.

"While we do your hair, Iris, I think I should tell you a story."

Chapter 17

I stood on the cliff face and waited to die. The high winds blew off the sea and whipped the folds of my robe up around me. It was my best robe, the one I was to have been married in, but it would do as well for my funeral. I didn't blame my father. He had merely obeyed the prophecy. Sacrifice a daughter to save a kingdom: It was an easy choice. I was raised to be a dutiful daughter, would never have dreamed of disobeying.

But it was hard to wait for death. I was only seventeen years old. I looked out over the ocean and tried to see the sea monster in the foamy wine-dark waves. I wondered if I should just jump. Perhaps it would be better to get it over with.

It wasn't my fault. I hadn't asked to be beautiful. Still less had I asked anyone to worship me. First it was a peasant, coming to me in the middle of the night and begging for my blessing to heal her warts. Soon they were crying out my name in childbirth. They carved statues of me and paraded them through the streets, showering them with rose petals, dousing them with sweet wine mixed with milk. Then the sea monster came and ravaged our lands till there was barely a fertile field left, barely a seaworthy ship. When my father consulted the oracle, the answer was harsh and clear: "Aphrodite is the goddess of beauty and will suffer no mortal girl to be placed above her. To appease the monster's appetite, you must sacrifice Psyche. Leave her to die on the high cliffs facing the sea."

So there I stood, waiting. The wailing of my sisters long gone, I leaned into the wind and fell.

But Eros saw me and his heart filled with love. He spoke to the wind: "Zephyr, lift up that maiden. Veil yourself in fog, so that my mother does not see, and carry her into the valley. I will build a palace there for her. Hurry, before the monster comes. And be gentle. Treat her like a newborn cloud out for her first shower."

Zephyr is the gentlest of all winds. I had plummeted halfway down the cliff face, when I stopped suddenly. I floated for a moment and then began to drift over the sea, going far, far away to a warm, green valley. The wind set me down and whispered in my ear, "Farewell, lovely Psyche. Your lord awaits you in that palace ahead. Do not be afraid."

"My lord?" I said. "Do you mean the monster? The one who was supposed to kill me?"

I could hear the smile in Zephyr's voice as he replied, "There will be no more monsters, Psyche. This is your husband's castle." Everything about Eros's palace was perfect and pleasing. When I saw it, I had a giddy feeling in my heart, like waking up and knowing it is your birthday. I could feel that somebody wonderful was waiting for me inside that house. As soon as I walked inside, I smelled something delicious and realized how long it had been since I'd eaten. Like a hungry animal, I followed the smell and found myself in a dining room with a shining wooden table and one chair.

Covered silver platters floated through the air. A napkin unfolded in midair and draped itself across my lap. Wine poured itself into a glass. I saw every kind of delicacy imaginable. There was a huge roast duck with apricot-cornbread stuffing. As I noticed it, a carving knife flew through the air and cut off the drumstick, my favorite part. Whenever I noticed a dish and thought it looked good, a portion of the dish would float onto my plate. There were hot creamy noodles with cheese and sweet peas; a salad of flowers and grapes; huge shrimp wrapped in bacon; wild mushrooms; dumplings filled with chicken and chestnuts; spicy fried sweet potatoes; corn pudding; and the most delicious wild onions—so sweet you could eat them like apples.

Just when I thought I couldn't eat anymore, all the food cleared itself away. I heard water splash in the other room as the dishes washed themselves. A voice spoke in my ear, "This way to your bedroom, my lady." I spun around, but there was no one there! "Straight ahead, my lady, and up the stairs. We have drawn you a hot bath."

I climbed the broad stairs to my bedroom, where invisible hands undressed me and helped me into a silver tub filled with steaming lavender-scented water. They scrubbed me until I gleamed, washed my hair, and cleaned behind my ears. After I was dried and rubbed all over with sweet almond oil, the invisible hands led me to bed and blew out the candles.

That night, a man came to me in the darkness. There was not the slightest ray of moon or starlight coming into the chamber to betray our faces to each other. In the darkness we could talk like old friends without worrying about what anyone looked like. He said that he loved me and that he had brought me there to be his bride. Of course, I was curious about how he looked, but my new husband told me that I could never look at him. He said it was the one thing between us that was forbidden.

"Ask for anything else, my Psyche, and you shall have it."

But there was nothing else I wanted. He felt and sounded so gentle and good that I didn't care at all what he looked like. I stayed there with him in his castle, and we were very happy.

But there was something missing. My new life felt so disconnected from my old one that it almost seemed like a dream. Sometimes I wondered if I really had died on that cliff facing the sea—if all the rest since then was just the crazy invention of a dying mind. All the details of my new life seemed to support my fear. Who has ever heard of invisible servants? And my husband only came at night. It was all so strange, and so lonely.

I asked him if I could go visit my family.

"Just to let them know that I am all right. They must be so sad thinking I have been killed by the sea monster."

"Psyche, they don't deserve your attention. Things are perfect here as they are. Why leave me for even one night to go see people unworthy of you?"

"But they are not unworthy; they are my family!"

"Your sisters secretly rejoice at your absence. They were always jealous of your beauty. Your father is a good man but lacked the bravery to save you. Stay with me, Psyche. I am all the family you need."

But I would not listen, and I begged him with such emotion that he was forced to let me go. I covered him with kisses, thanking him and promising to be careful. The next afternoon, Zephyr set me down on the highest tower of my father's castle. Everyone was amazed to see me, especially my sisters. I told them about everything: the food; the lush gardens; the castle, which had the best of everything; and most of all, I spoke of the goodness of my husband. My sisters' eyes gleamed when they heard about all the luxury I was enjoying. I was too innocent to see their jealousy or to hear anything but honest concern in their questions to me.

"But, Sister, you say you have never seen him. How can this be?"

"Oh, he has forbidden it. He comes only at night."

"But why?" said Eleutheria.

"Yes," cried Tamakloe, "why the need for such extreme, such guilty secrecy?"

"Well, I don't know." I felt suddenly ashamed for my husband. I had never even wondered why he had forbidden me to see him. "It—it is what he wants, so I never thought to ask. And, you know, I always used to dream of meeting my suitors in the darkness, so they could not—you know—be so influenced by my looks. So they could appreciate me for who I am inside, my external beauty hidden."

My sisters exchanged an angry look to hear me mention my beauty. I regretted having spoken of it. I could tell that I looked better than ever—I wore my happiness like a halo—and I did not wish to gloat.

"Dear, dear Psyche," said Tamakloe. "The darkness has not been arranged by this man to hide you, but to hide him."

"Yes," said Eleutheria. "It doesn't make sense. Any normal man would wish the lights to be brighter so that he could see the famous beauty of the woman he had won. Depend upon it, he has something to hide. Imagine if he is really that same sea monster who has ravaged our lands. Imagine how hideous he might be."

"Perhaps one day he will eat you," offered Tamakloe.

I reassured them. I told them that I was absolutely sure of my husband's goodness. He felt, sounded, and behaved like a prince. He could not be a monster. But the seed of doubt had been planted in my heart.

When I said good-bye to them, my sisters cried, and Tamakloe whispered in my ear as she embraced me, "Oh, do be careful, Sister, in case he eats you."

I was not at peace that night with my husband, but I hid it well. I waited until I heard his breathing slow down. I whispered to him, "My love?" But there was no answer. I lay there for a moment and thought about all his kindness to me. Was this how I repaid him, by breaking the only promise he had asked of me? I resolved not to do it. I couldn't sleep that night, wondering what lay beside me.

My resolve lasted that one night. The next, I hid an oil lamp under the bed. When I heard his breathing become thick and regular, I slipped off the bed and reached for the lamp and tinderbox. My hands shook as I lit it, listening all the time to the breath of my sleeping husband. I held the lamp above the bed—and gasped.

He was beautiful. Oh, Iris, he was the most beautiful man I had ever seen. He lay sleeping half on his back and half curled on his side. Great white wings were folded under him and blond curls spilled over his soft, rosy skin. I bent closer to look at the face that I had kissed thousands of times. My lips silently mouthed, "I love you, Eros," for I knew then who my husband really was. But as I bent in close, a single drop of hot oil fell from my lamp and landed on Eros's white shoulder.

He hissed in pain and opened his eyes. I started back, guilty. Eros met my eyes. There was no surprise in his, only sorrow. Without a word, he got up and flew away. With him went all the joy I had ever felt in my life. I tried to fly away after him. I leaped out of the window with my arms opened wide, only to fall flat on my face in the dust. I lay there facedown for what seemed like hours. When the sun set, I got up from the dust, to find that the castle was gone. I didn't know what to do. I was cold. I cried.

At some point I decided to start walking. It was the only thing I could think of to do. I walked until my knees and hips ached, until my feet were huge blisters and there were strips of pain running along my shins. I stopped to sleep in hollows at the side of the road. I ate what I could scavenge or beg. People no longer marveled at my beauty. My face was hollow with grief, stained with dust and tears.

The biggest problem with being homeless is the boredom.

When you have nowhere to go, every day feels so long. I spoke to no one, except to beg. I did nothing except walk and think about the mistake I had made. Everything reminded me of Eros. I thought about him so much that I began to go a little crazy. I whispered, "I love you, Eros," and, "I'm sorry," over and over.

One day I came to a temple of Demeter. My first thought when I saw the tiny temple was: "Perhaps that is where my husband has gone." When I entered, I saw that it was a terrible mess inside. There were sheaves of grain scattered everywhere, and scythes and bags of seed. I began to clean the temple. In my muddled mind I thought that I would make it nice and neat for my husband when he came home. I sorted out the wheat from the oats. I laid the farming tools in neat stacks on the floor. I was happy to be working, and the silence in the temple and the sweet smell of the grain soothed me.

I fell asleep on the temple floor, with my head on a sack of barley. That night I dreamed of the goddess Demeter. She laid a hand on my forehead and said, "Dear girl, your act of pious labor has moved me. You seek to regain your husband's love, but it is not he that must be appeased. You must seek out his mother, that powerful goddess whom you have offended. Perhaps through humbling yourself and begging forgiveness, you may convince her of your worth. Go to her temple and submit yourself to her judgment."

I made the long journey to Aphrodite's main temple. I laid down the garland of flowers I had brought, and I prostrated myself at the statue's feet.

"Dear Goddess, I never wanted people to worship me. I

never wanted to offend you. I only want your son's love back. Please tell me what I can do. I made you a garland of flowers; it is all I have."

The temple was filled with the sound of scornful laughter, and she answered me, "So, now you come sniveling and begging, wanting my help? Now you do me the honor that you should have done long ago? You are beneath my notice! Look at you, worshipped as a great beauty—you have rags for clothes and lice in your hair. Who are you that I should help you?"

"I am Psyche. I am your daughter."

"You are no daughter of mine. Your husband does not want you. He has cast you off because you could not obey the one command he gave you. He is still in bed, recovering from the burn you gave him."

"Please, Goddess, I am so sorry. Please, I love him so much."

"We shall see. Since you no longer have any beauty to boast of, perhaps my son will take you back as a maid. Why don't you show me how well you can clean."

I felt rough hands pick me up by the hair and drag me toward the temple door. The pain was horrible. The next thing I knew, I was facedown on a hard stone floor. Aphrodite was before me, covered in a golden halo, a cruel expression on her lovely face as she gestured to the sides of the room.

"These seeds are food for my pet doves. Sort them for me. I am off to a party at Dionysus's palace, which will last all night. When I come back in the morning, I expect each seed in its own pile."

She turned around and strode out, her golden mantle billowing around her. As she left, she threw something over her shoulder, laughing. "Dinner."

I picked it up. It was a loaf of brown bread, halfway covered with mold. I looked around. I was in a large storehouse filled with huge mountains of grain. There were seeds of every kind, all mixed together in heaps. I sat there frozen. I didn't know where to begin. Even if I worked for the rest of my life, I could barely make a dent. I began to cry.

There was a tickling on my foot, and I looked down to see a line of tiny black ants crawling across me. "hello psyche don't cry" they sang out in a quiet chorus.

"Hello, ant friends. I'm sorry for crying, but I just don't know how I'll ever sort it all out," I said.

"we will help you we love to work"

I watched in amazed gratitude as the little ants trooped to and fro in neat lines, carrying the seeds on their backs. There were thousands and thousands of ants, and among them, they made short work of the gargantuan task. When they were done, I broke up the good part of the bread into little crumbs for them. I was too happy to eat.

"yum we love crumbs"

"Thank you, ant friends."

When Aphrodite came back from the party, she found me asleep on the threshing-room floor, surrounded by sorted grain. Not a seed was out of place. She kicked me in the side.

"Get up, you lazy girl. I know you had some kind of help for this. But it doesn't matter. Come with me." She smiled cruelly. I got up and followed her. She took me for a long journey *through the clouds in her swan-drawn chariot. We landed on a beautiful island. "Do you see those golden rams?" She pointed her fan in the direction of a meadow just beyond a nearby river.*

"I want you to gather fleece for me from each one of the rams. From each one! I will return tomorrow morning." As she spun around and remounted her chariot, I heard her murmur, "I'll return for your body."

I walked toward the meadow and stood at the bank of the river, gazing across at the rams. The field was rimmed with high hedges. In front of them, the rams wandered about, eating grass. They were beautiful, noble beasts. Their fleece shone in the sun. I called out, "Hello, ram friends. Hello! I need to gather some of your wool." I pictured wandering among them, patting their heads and gathering their soft, gleaming wool. This would be easy.

At the sound of my voice, one of the rams galloped to the edge of the river and growled. His mouth dripped with foam. He seemed to be trying to figure out how to swim across the river and gore me. I saw that my task would not be as easy as I thought. A few other rams noticed me, and soon a tiny flock was gathered at the shore, making horrible sounds and pawing the ground. Although I knew they could not swim the river, which was deep and swift-flowing, I was terrified.

Suddenly all the rams turned their backs to me. A little brown rabbit had begun to hop across the meadow. All at once, they pounced. I turned my head away, unable to watch. It was terrible what they did to that rabbit.

I didn't know what to do. They would certainly kill me if I tried to take their wool. I might not even make it across the river, I realized, as I tested it with one foot. It was running faster than any river I had ever seen. I put one foot in and then another. I might as well die trying, *I thought.*

"Poor Psyche," said a deep, kind baritone that came from the water. "I am the river god Geleus. I want to help you, Psyche. Do not approach the rams during the day, for the sun fills them with insane blood thirst. At night my waters will lower to let you cross. The rams will have gone away to sleep, but you can collect their wool from where it has clung to the branches of the tall hedges surrounding the meadow."

I thanked Geleus. When night came, I did just as he advised, and I came back with my arms full of golden wool. Aphrodite was shocked to see me the next morning.

"You wicked girl. Someone has been helping you again. Well, it doesn't matter, for this next task will definitely get rid of you. Here." She handed me a little box made of cedarwood with golden fastenings. "There is another party tomorrow, and I am feeling worn-out from tending to my sick son. My hair is not as lustrous as usual, and my eyes lack finesse. Take this box down to Persephone in hell. Tell her that Aphrodite would like to borrow some of her beauty. Bring me back the box before tomorrow evening."

With that, Aphrodite was off. I wept again. No one could help me this time. How would I ever get down to hell? I didn't know the way. I sat there for some time in confusion and despair. Then I made a decision. The only way I could get to hell in time was to die.

I filled my pockets with rocks and waded into the river. I

117

walked out to the deepest part, where the water was higher than my head, and I let the rocks pull me down. It was hard to do. When I got underwater, I tried to breathe in the water and relax. Just as I began to go limp, a hand lifted me up by the collar and dragged me back into the air. It was a large, green-skinned man with a beard made of water. He looked angry.

"Child, what are you doing? Do you think I would let you drown yourself in me? After the way I helped you with those rams, is this the thanks I get?" He took the stones out of my pockets and clapped me on the back.

"Geleus"—I coughed—"I am doomed. I need to go to hell."

"You don't need to die to get there, you silly thing. Are you going to give up now, after how far you've come? You need to keep on living so you can find your love."

"Okay, Geleus. Tell me what to do."

He gave me directions for the long journey, then told me how to dip a piece of bread in the river Styx and throw it to Cerberus, the three-headed dog, so he would allow me to pass. He told me not to eat any of the food they gave me in hell, but to take the box from Persephone and leave. But above all, he cautioned me not to open the box. I thanked him and kissed his watery beard.

His directions were perfect. I soon found myself before hell's three-headed guard dog, Cerberus. He was letting all the dead souls into hell, but when I approached, he bared three mouths full of teeth and barred my passage. He was horribly ugly and fierce, with patches of mangy pink skin showing through his gray fur. I pulled the Styx-dipped bread out of my pocket and threw it to him. He gobbled it up and fell asleep immediately.

The facade of Hades' palace slowly came into view. It was a grim, majestic building of granite and black marble. I gathered my courage and fought my way in through the hordes of shades that were begging the guards for entry. The guards seemed unsurprised to see me. When I told them I was there to see Persephone, they nodded and waved me in. A huge vaulted ceiling rose above me, decorated with a blue and gold mosaic of the zodiac signs. To my sides were rows of black marble columns blazing with purple flames. A bloodred carpet cut through the center, leading to the raised dais where the king and queen of hell sat in state on their ruby thrones. I was filled with awe.

I walked slowly toward them, head bowed. Persephone was so lovely. It was easy to see why Aphrodite would choose to borrow beauty from her. She sat up very straight in her chair and watched the hall as if she were dreaming. With her lovely, pale face she was like a woman carved out of ice. Hades sat at her side, radiating power. I bowed down before them and spoke loudly so that my voice would shake less.

"Mighty Queen Persephone, my mistress Aphrodite sends me to beg a favor of you. She says that she has grown tired from tending to her sick son, who is my own beloved Eros." I raised my eyes to the goddess's sad, shining face and felt a stab of jealousy at the thought of how devoted Hades was to his wife. If only Eros were as devoted to me. I closed my eyes. "Aphrodite wishes for some of your beauty, of which I see you have so much. She gave me this box, to carry it."

I placed the box on the ground and waited in silence. My heart was pounding. What if Persephone were angry with my request? I raised my eyes again to hers.

She smiled. It was a funny sort of smile that left her eyes sad. She said, "Ah, Psyche, you remind me a little of myself, when I was young and foolish. You are welcome here, and I will fill the box with what your mistress wants. She has already given me instructions. But stay with us for a while. Sit in a throne by my side and feast with me tonight. I rarely have visitors."

But I remembered Geleus's advice and turned down Persephone's offer as politely as I could. I didn't eat anything that night, and I slept on the ground at the foot of the thrones. I woke up covered in sweat, and dust from the floor, and gazed out the window. In the distance I saw poor Sisyphus, doomed to push his heavy boulder up a hill for eternity. Soon shades of the dead began to gather in the hall, whispering to themselves. A hurricane of complaints filled my ears. "It was all a mistake Persephone the dark queen I am too young I can't find my son Hades it's so ugly here I can't remember my name where did all my gold go my cat died in the fire I am so hungry so bored there are no trees here I miss my mommy." They pushed each other out of the way, jockeying for the best spot in the hall.

A hush came over the shades as the heralds of hell entered, blowing their long golden trumpets. Then Hades and Persephone appeared and took their seats. Persephone was carrying the box. She saw me and waved me forward. It did not look like one drop of beauty had been taken away from her.

"Here you are, Psyche." She placed the box in my hands and met my eyes. Hers were such a pale blue, they seemed translucent. For a second I thought I saw flowers in her irises. The flowers blossomed and closed, blossomed and closed. "I have

put into this box exactly what Aphrodite asked of me. Do you understand?"

I nodded. I was too dazzled by the flowers in her eyes to notice what she was saying.

"Good. Bring this box straight back to your mistress. Take the high road; it is faster. My guard will show you the way."

"Thank you, Your Majesty." I bowed low.

"Good luck, Psyche," said a great, deep voice. I looked up at Hades. He smiled at me and reached out to pat my head, saying, "Little butterfly."

The guard was a ghost named Orpheus, with a sad, unkind face. He held a lyre under one arm, but did not play it. He led me silently toward the upper world. After hours of walking, he turned to look back at me, then asked, "What's in the box?"

"Some of Persephone's beauty."

"Hah!" he replied in an angry voice. "Life is wasted on mortals. You always do the one forbidden thing."

I didn't know what he was talking about or why he was so angry. We went on walking in silence. After a while longer, he stopped and said, "I've got to get back to my wife, Eurydice." When he said her name, his face lit up for a moment, and it was like a ray of sun breaking out on a cold gray day. "You can find your way back from here." He looked at the box, then said in a sarcastic voice, "And whatever you do, don't open the box."

I continued on alone and soon reached the sunlight. As I stepped into the light, I thought of the radiant look on the ghost's face when he mentioned his wife's name. If only Eros looked like that when he said my name! Perhaps Aphrodite was right, I thought, perhaps he no longer loved me. I was so ragged and dirty.

The box felt heavy in my hands. It must be packed with loveliness, I thought. It was so full, maybe Aphrodite wouldn't notice if I took just a few drops to sprinkle on my face. I would get my glow back. Just a few drops. It would be just like when Eros first met me, before I messed everything up. He would love me again. Just a few drops.

When I opened the box, hundreds of sharp silver needles shot out and sank into my body. It was a trap. I sank to my knees. It hurt everywhere, horribly. Then the poison took effect, and the pain faded. I fell into a deep, stygian sleep.

In my sleep, I felt the needles being pulled out, one by one. I flailed my arms, but someone pinned them down. The slow torture continued.

"Shhh. My Psyche, suffer it. It will be over soon."

I opened my eyes. It was Eros! His wound had healed, and he looked even more handsome in the sunlight than he had by the light of my lamp. He was pulling out the needles with his teeth.

"Eros." I began to cry.

He spit out the last needle and smiled. Then he lifted me up in his arms and flew with me to heaven. He flew me all the way to Zeus's palace, which was ten times as grand as Hades'. The light that came off Zeus and Hera was so bright that I had to close my eyes and bury my face in my husband's shoulder. I heard him speak in a brave, proud voice.

"Father Zeus, I want you to meet my wife, Psyche. Please don't ever let us be apart again. Tell my mother to be reconciled to her. Make Psyche immortal, and let nothing but pleasure come from our union."

Zeus spoke in a voice that made my ears ring. "CHILD, COME HERE AND DRINK."

Eros set me down amid the blinding golden light. A cup was pressed to my lips, and I drank the nectar of immortality.

Chapter 18

Psyche had just finished her story when there was a big, thumping knock on the door, as though someone were hitting it with a slab of meat.

"Oh dear," said Aphrodite. "My husband has come to ruin all the fun." She took a small compact out of her pocket and examined her face in it, smoothing out her eyebrows. "Come in, dear," she trilled.

The door opened and the smell of diesel fuel filled the room. Hephaestus was so huge that he had to duck through the doorway. He was dressed in bright orange overalls splattered with grease and soot. Kind eyes twinkled at Iris behind a pair of plastic goggles above a profusion of black beard.

"Hephaestus, darling, how many times have I told you to shower before you come to the salon? And take off those ridiculous goggles. And your beard has run amok again!" Aphrodite regarded him with an expression of distaste. Hephaestus moved the goggles to the top of his head and grinned, his teeth very white against the black beard.

"You see, child," he said, nodding to Iris, "my wife never stops trying to make me presentable. But I have always been a grease monkey, and I will always be one. You can't teach an old dog new tricks. And Aphrodite and I are very, very old dogs."

Aphrodite lifted her nose in the air. "Hmph! An old dog! You know just what to say to a woman to make her feel special, Hephaestus."

"I did not come here to flirt with you, Aphrodite. I came to say hello to the girl, and to give her a gift for her father."

"Fine, then, give it to her. I suppose it is some rusty auto part or something." Aphrodite picked a pair of golden tweezers off the counter and began plucking her eyebrows.

Hephaestus winked at Iris. He lurched across the room toward her, knocking over a crystal candleholder, two vases, and a large hair-color display. Psyche seemed used to it. She followed behind him with a dustbin.

"I have this limp," Hephaestus explained to Iris, "ever since I tried to get between my father and mother when they were fighting. Zeus threw me halfway across the world. But don't worry; he's calmed down a lot in the last thousand years."

Iris thought about her mom and dad's bickering. "Yeah, I think it's best to stay out of it when parents are fighting."

"Absolutely. Oh, here. I thought this might come in

handy." He reached into his pocket and pulled out something round, gray, and sticky.

Iris turned it over in her hands. "Is this what I think it is, Hephaestus?"

"Yup." He smiled proudly. "Duct tape! The perfect gift for the father who has everything."

"But it's not my father's birthday, or anything. Why would I give him a gift?"

"When you visit him, bring it. Best to come bearing gifts."

Iris looked at the tape in confusion. She certainly hoped that she wouldn't have to visit her father anytime soon. She had only been to Wisconsin once, when she was seven. Her father had made her camp out the whole time in a tent in the backyard because his wife believed children were contagious.

"Well, okay, Hephaestus. The next time I see him, I'll be sure to give him this. Thank you."

Aphrodite snorted. "Duct tape? You're giving her duct tape?"

Hephaestus narrowed his eyes. "No ordinary duct tape. This is my special proprietary brand, blessed by Hephaestus. Duct tape fixes everything!"

"Except an overgrown beard and garage odor," murmured Aphrodite.

"What was that?" said Hephaestus.

"Oh, nothing."

"Well, Iris, I'd best get back to my workshop. I'm trying

to modify a '57 Chevy so that real flames come out of the tailpipe and you can grill burgers over them as you drive."

"Wow, that sounds cool."

"Yeah, I wish *some* people thought so." He rolled his eyes toward his wife, who was powdering her nose.

"All right, bye then, everyone!" Hephaestus turned to go, but Aphrodite cleared her throat noisily.

He turned back around and smiled. "Yes, dearest?"

Aphrodite cocked her head to expose one cheek. "You may kiss me now."

"Oh! *May* I, really?"

"Yes, you may." She looked hurt. "After all, I *am* the goddess of love, you know. Most men would kill for the privilege."

Hephaestus limped over to her and took her in his arms. He spoke in a different voice than before: "My beautiful swan. My tidal wave." He smoothed her hair. "Do you know, I think I am the luckiest man on Olympus to have such a bride! Iris, Psyche?"

They turned their backs. After a minute Hephaestus left, and Aphrodite bustled about looking happy and embarrassed, a large grease smudge on her cheek.

"My husband! He always spoils all the fun." But Iris didn't believe her for a moment.

The door jingled and Eros entered. He looked triumphant. "Iris, that was a stroke of genius. It's too early to say for sure, but I think love is in the air. When I left them, the gentleman in question was cooking his lady a lobster feast." Eros scooped up Psyche and danced her around the room. "Ah, what fun it is to be me!"

"Bravo, dear," said Aphrodite. "It's been a very successful day." She spun Iris around to face the mirror. Iris almost didn't recognize herself. Her hair was glossy and shiny and streaked with blond and red. It was flashier than anything Iris had ever done to her hair, but she liked it.

"Thanks, Aphrodite!"

"It's my pleasure, child." Aphrodite handed her the silver boxes—which Iris certainly would never open now—and her clothes and backpack. "You come back and see us whenever you need love or beauty advice. It's free of charge—"

Just then Aphrodite's swirly pink clock struck seven. Iris's mother got up at seven! Iris unfurled the rainbow and was back in bed in seconds, feigning sleep and wondering what Aphrodite had been saying. When the clock had cut her off, she was saying something that sounded an awful lot like *It's free of charge to family.*

Chapter 19

When Iris came out to the breakfast table, Helen gasped.

"Iris, you look fabulous!"

"Thanks, Mom."

"Your hair! It's glowing! And your skin looks, I don't know, kind of sparkly."

"Thanks, Mom." Iris began to make up a story to cover it, but her mother took care of that for her.

Helen nodded knowingly. "A few weeks ago, I added more vitamin E to your daily vitamins. That must be it. Very good for the skin and hair, you know."

"Yeah, Mom. That must be it."

Helen sighed. It was a long, sad sigh, and Iris studied her, worried. This would be the first day she could remember that her mother wouldn't go to work. What would she do all day?

"Are you all right, Mom?"

Helen smiled. "I'm fine, Iris."

Iris wanted to give Helen all the money she'd earned at Apollo's club, but she knew it would look suspicious. She would have to wait until later that day so she could say she'd gone to a garage sale and sold the jazz albums there.

"Hey, Mom?"

"Yeah."

"Why don't we go out for breakfast today. We can get breakfast burritos. Just to sort of cheer us up."

The mention of burritos perked Helen up, as Iris had known it would. Her mother loved burritos more than anything.

"That's a great idea, Iris!" They headed out to the Sentra, and ten minutes later, Helen was leaning into a giant sombrero and shouting, "TWO BEANTASTIC BREAKFAST BURRITOS, PLEASE. NO SOUR CREAM. WE BROUGHT OUR OWN SOY SOUR CREAM FROM HOME. IT HAS ISOFLAVONES. AND ONE COFFEE AND ONE ORANGE JUICE."

Iris tugged on her mother's sleeve. "I want a coffee, too."

"Since when do you drink coffee? MAKE THAT TWO COFFEES, PLEASE."

"I don't know. I guess I just got a taste for it." The truth was, the sleepless night was beginning to catch up with Iris. She felt sort of droopy.

Through a burst of static, the sombrero replied, "TURKMENISTAN TACO, TACO, TACO, WINSTON CHURCHILL CINNAMON CRISPAS?"

Iris's mother replied, "NO, THANK YOU, WE DO NOT WANT

CINNAMON CRISPAS. THEY HAVE TRANS FAT IN THEM, WHICH CAUSES CANCER."

The sombrero replied, "*GÖTTERDÄMMERUNG* $6.99. BEETHOVEN *JAI ALAI* TACO, TACO, TACO! P. DIDDY AND HAVE A NICE DAY."

They pulled up to the burro to wait. Taco, Taco, Taco! was Helen's favorite restaurant, due to the unexpected excellence of their $1.99 bean burritos. In a few moments, the burro's head opened. A hand appeared, deposited two paper bags into the Nissan, and disappeared again into the metal beast. The fragrance of hot tortillas filled the little car, and Iris's mother sighed with happiness. They pulled into their favorite space in the parking lot to eat—the one that faced the piñata-shaped topiary—and spread the paper wrappers on their laps.

Helen took a bite. "Ah, delicious as always. You know, Iris, when I've got a good bean burrito on my lap, I feel like nothing can stop me!"

"That's the spirit, Mom!"

Helen continued between bites, "I've got a long day ahead of me, Iris. I'm going around to some different labs today. I, well, I just want to see what kind of opportunities they're offering for soybeantologists. I haven't been so happy at Tofu-licious lately."

Iris tried to look surprised. "I'm sorry to hear that, Mom."

"Yeah, well, maybe it's a good thing. I mean, it's about time I looked around and saw what else is out there, don't you think?"

"Yeah, Mom. Anyone would be lucky to have you. You know more about soybeans than anyone."

Helen smiled and swiped at the hot sauce dripping down her chin. "I *do* know a lot about my field."

"Yeah, you even won that award."

"I did! The Golden Nodule! For outstanding research in nitrogen fixation." Helen's eyes became dreamy. "Ah, those were the days, Iris. Back in grad school, when I didn't have any managers looking over my shoulders, talking about efficiency and profit. Back then, it was all about the soybeans."

"Well, maybe that could happen again, Mom. What if you started your own business, like based on all the research you've done. Then you could be your own boss."

"Starting up a business takes money, Iris."

"Well, what if you *had* a lot of money. What if . . . you *won* it, like in the lottery or something?"

Helen smiled sadly. "Nobody ever wins the lottery." She stuffed the last of the burrito into her mouth and started the car. "We'd better get going or you'll be late for school."

Iris sighed. She had been hoping to be late. Her first period was biology with Mrs. Webb, and she had a bad feeling about it.

Chapter 20

When Iris walked into biology, her teacher stabbed her with a sterile lance.

"*Ow!*" Iris glared at Mrs. Webb, who handed her some gauze.

"Now, dear, it's all for the good of science." She smeared Iris's blood on a microscope slide. "Class, we're analyzing our blood today. We will be looking at it through a microscope and testing its type. Extra credit will be awarded for anyone who finds anything *unusual* in their sample."

Mrs. Webb was a strange choice for a biology teacher, because she believed the planet Earth was a science project created by aliens, like a large Ant Farm. She wore the same sweat suit to school every day. It was black velour, emblazoned with airbrushed alien heads and Egyptian pyramids. Mrs. Webb always managed to work aliens into any project they did. Iris was getting an awful grade in the class, because she couldn't see alien heads in fossils or hear alien voices over the ham radio. None of the other students could, either, of course, but they went along with the program.

Mrs. Webb drew a picture of a flying saucer on the board. "The average human red blood cell is shaped like this. Coincidence? It's up to you to find out."

Iris rolled her eyes. Her adventures with the gods had given her less patience for the kind of nonsense that went on in her classes. Also, she was sleep-deprived, which made her irritable. She raised her hand. Mrs. Webb frowned.

"Yes, Iris?"

"My mother said red blood cells are shaped that way to give them more surface area for gasses to be passed back and forth, because that's the main thing red blood cells do is transport—"

Mrs. Webb interrupted her. "Yes, well, I know your mother has some strange beliefs. We had an amusing talk on Career Day. She actually thinks humans are descended from monkeys!" The class laughed dutifully. "But what can you expect from someone who devotes her life to seaweed?"

"Soybeans!"

"Whatever." Mrs. Webb turned to the class. "As I was saying, after we test the blood type, we will examine the cells under the microscope. Draw a picture of what you see, and keep an eye out for anything unusual, such as an alien signature on the cell walls."

But Iris was mad now. She raised her hand again.

"Yes, Iris?" Mrs. Webb's voice was cold.

"Membranes."

"I beg your pardon, Iris?"

"Animal cells have membranes. Only plant cells have cell walls. What kind of biology teacher *are* you, anyway, if you don't even know about *cells?*"

The class drew in a collective breath at Iris's daring.

"Well, I may not know as much about cells as your mother, the seaweed expert," said Mrs. Webb, looking in her grade book, "but I do know my arithmetic. And nine detentions plus one detention equals"—Mrs. Webb paused dramatically—"one *visit to the principal.*"

The class let out an *oooh* of excitement and horror. Iris's stomach lurched. She hunched down in her seat, deflated. What had she been thinking, talking back to her teacher like that? The gods weren't with her here.

And she had an appointment that very afternoon to see Athena and Artemis. What if the principal kept her so late that she missed the meeting?

The principal! She had often wondered who was crazy enough to hire the teachers at Erebus. But she had wondered this the same way she wondered which was worse, freezing to death or being burned alive: She didn't really want to know the answer.

Chapter 21

When Iris opened the door to the office, a huge German shepherd leaped at her. Foam dripped from his open mouth.

"Down, boy!"

The woman who had spoken was enormous and wore a black housedress and curlers. She ripped a piece off a glazed doughnut, dunked it in some coffee, and threw it to the dog. He ate it and fell asleep.

"You may enter now," the woman said.

"Thank you." Iris stepped over the sleeping dog. The secretary turned up the volume on her TV. Some kind of exercise program was on that involved violent movements. A muscular man in a tight purple jumpsuit was kicking the air, while perky music played. The secretary sat and watched, chewing on her doughnut.

"Um, excuse me," said Iris, "but I was supposed to see the principal."

"The principal is busy with another problem student right now. You will wait." Iris sighed and eyed the dough-nuts. She did not like being called a problem student. It was the teachers that were the problem.

A hollow voice crackled over the intercom: "Chair of Discomfort: three thirty-seven."

The secretary reached into her drawer and pulled out a big chart filled with lots of rows and columns. She entered a figure on it and put it back. The door to the principal's office opened and a boy staggered out. He was panting with fatigue and clutching his stomach.

"Don't let me hear about any more spitballs," rang out the hollow voice from within. The boy wove his way across the room, whimpering.

The secretary selected a new doughnut, a Boston Kreme, which she waved in the direction of the principal's door. Iris stepped in. Inside his windowless office, the principal slumped in a red leather La-Z-Boy in the center of the room. He had pale skin, and dark circles under his eyes, which made him look as though he had not slept for a very long time. He wore a wrinkled tuxedo with a bloodred cummerbund, and a Daily Planner hung from his neck on a black velvet ribbon.

The huge desk in front of him was completely empty except for one of those paperweights with the swinging metal balls. Two balls swung off each side, making an ominous metallic click.

"Problem child, please stand in the corner and hold the cinder block."

"What?" said Iris, startled.

"STAND IN THE CORNER AND HOLD THE CINDER BLOCK. Hold it until I tell you to put it down."

Iris looked in the corner. Red tape marked an X on the floor. On it sat a gray cinder block with dripping blood-red letters painted on the side: **CindeR blOck oF puNish-MenT.** It looked heavy. Iris walked over and lifted up the cinder block. It was even heavier than it looked.

"Now, stand on the X and think about how heavy a burden on our schools are its problem children. You are on the clock for five minutes." He pulled out a stopwatch.

Iris felt her palms begin to sweat and make pasty pools on the side of the cinder block. Her lower back hurt. This was awful. She thought she remembered something in the Declaration of Independence about cruel and unusual punishment being wrong. Or maybe it was the Constitution. She wasn't sure, though, that these documents applied to schoolchildren.

"One minute down! Continue to contemplate your perfidy!"

Iris's arm muscles were twitching, and the pain in her fingers was horrible. She wondered, through the pain, what *perfidy* meant.

"I can't hold it any longer. I'm sorry." She dropped the cinder block, and it fell to the floor with an awful thud that set the metal balls swinging again on the principal's desk.

He hit the stopwatch. It chirped and a computerized voice said, "One. Minute. Sixteen. Seconds."

"Not bad for a girl," said the principal. He hit the intercom button and yelled into it, "Cinder Block of Punishment: one sixteen."

"Okay," he continued, looking at Iris, "open the closet door." Iris did as he said, stepping back in case another German shepherd was inside. But she found with relief only an empty closet with an inflatable kiddie pool on the floor. The pool was shark-shaped and empty. A sign on it said **sHaRK oF desPair.**

"Here," said the principal, holding out something small and white. Earlier that year, Erebus's school cafeteria had switched from separate forks and spoons to the compact two-in-one "spork." This particular spork, however, had been tampered with. A hole had been drilled in the bottom of the spoon part, and small red letters on the stem said **spoRk of futiLitY.**

"There is a water fountain down the hall. Take the Spork of Futility and use it to carry water from the fountain into the Shark of Despair. I want to see that shark overflowing. Now go."

"But the water will spill out the hole," said Iris. She did not understand what the principal was up to. Perhaps he was insane.

"Oh, the water will spill out the hole? Do you really think so?" he said in a mocking voice. "OF COURSE THE WATER WILL LEAK OUT!" he shrieked. "THAT'S

THE WHOLE POINT." He ran a hand through his hair and reached out to set a metal ball swinging. He spoke again, in a calmer tone. "Problem student, in case you don't know what *futility* means, you will soon learn. And as you try to fill the empty shark with the flawed spork, you will please contemplate how you will ever fill your empty mind with knowledge if you keep misbehaving in class. Disobedience is the hole in the spork of education! NOW BEGIN!" He hit the stopwatch again.

When Iris got to the fountain, she realized that she was terribly thirsty, probably from holding up that cinder block. She pushed the button and the water flowed out in a smooth, inviting arc. When she bent down to drink, however, the water shut off. She straightened back up, puzzled. She pressed the button. Again water arced out. She bent to drink, and again, as soon as the water seemed almost to touch her lips, it cut off. Weird. She looked above the water fountain and saw a sign: **FounTaiN of TantaliZatioN.** What was going on? She turned the water on again and held her spork under the stream. This time the fountain kept flowing, but, as Iris expected, all the water drained out of the hole as soon as she filled it. She didn't know what else to do, so she carried the wet, empty spork back to the principal's office and shook off a tiny drop into the kiddie pool. The principal ignored her.

"Excuse me, ma'am," Iris said to the secretary.

"Yes," said the enormous woman, her eyes not leaving the TV screen.

"I'm sorry to bother you, but the principal—I think there's something wrong with him. He's making me fill up a kiddie pool with a leaky spork."

"You think that's bad, wait until you sit in the Chair of Discomfort."

"But I think maybe there's something wrong with that man to make children do these things," said Iris. "He looks really tired. I think maybe he's on drugs. He's not like an ordinary principal."

"THERE IS NOTHING WRONG WITH MY HUS-BAND." The secretary's loud voice shocked Iris and woke up the dog, who immediately started gnawing off one of the desk's metal legs. "Cerberus, stop!" She dipped another piece of doughnut into the coffee and threw it to him. He ate it and fell back to sleep.

The dog's name confirmed what Iris had already begun to suspect. It suddenly made sense why all her teachers were so uniformly horrible. "I think I have something for you," Iris said as she pulled Aphrodite's box out of her bag and put it on the secretary's desk. The woman opened it.

"*Ooooo!* Facial glitter! Where did you get this?" Without waiting for an answer, the secretary dabbed it on her eyelids and lips. Iris was getting used to weird sights, but nothing could have prepared her for what happened next. Before her eyes, the secretary shrank. The triple chin became single and dainty. The huge belly became a tiny waist. The fat secretary was transformed into a glamorous beauty. She ripped off her housedress to reveal a black silk evening gown.

"Well, just in time for spring. This must be Aphrodite's balm. Who are you and how did you get it?"

"I'm Iris Greenwold, and I got it at the Swan Salon."

The secretary gasped. "*You've* been to the *Swan?*" She pressed the intercom button. "Hades, get out here. We have a situation."

The door opened and the principal shambled out. His tired eyes lit up when he saw the transformation in his wife. "Persephone, honey, you look great. What happened?"

Persephone fired back at him: "*She* gave it to me. Her name is apparently Iris Greenwold. Hades, you have been torturing a friend of the gods! Apologize to her this instant."

Hades' face fell, and Iris thought for a moment he might cry. "Iris," he stammered, "why didn't you tell me? Oh dear, this is very embarrassing. Please don't tell Zeus. Oh, here, please, let me take that." He took the spork from her. "Sit down. We're very, very glad you are here." He ran into his office and came back, pushing the recliner. "Persephone, give her a doughnut."

"Thank you," said Iris as she sank down into the poofy red leather. Cerberus woke up and eyed her doughnut, drool pooling between his paws. "I hope you don't mind my saying this, but I don't think you should make *anybody* do those cruel things, no matter who they are."

Hades pouted. "But we can't stop, Iris! Punishment is what we're *best* at. Middle school is the closest thing we've found to hell."

"Well," said Iris, chewing her doughnut and thinking.

"I'll make you a deal. I won't tell Zeus about the horrible torture you inflicted upon me, if you agree to stop making kids hold cinder blocks and sit on uncomfortable chairs. And if you try to hire nicer teachers." She was bluffing, of course, since she had no idea where Zeus was, but they didn't have to know that.

"Oh," Hades whined, "but the teachers we picked are the scariest ones we could *find*. We had to look all *over* for them."

"Why don't you hire some of the other gods?" Iris said. "Apollo would be a great music teacher, if he had the time to do it. And I think Dionysus would be awesome for chemistry, at least the part on fermentation. Then you guys would feel more at home."

Hades looked unconvinced. "That might be a good idea, but if we don't torture the kids, it will be so boring. What will we do to them when they come to our office?"

"Why don't you tell them a story instead? You gods know so many great stories."

"Hmm." Hades thought about it for a moment. "That's not a bad idea. We could tell them about Prometheus, whose organs were eaten out of him every morning by an eagle!"

"Or about Ixion," said Persephone excitedly. "Remember him, honey? You tied him onto a big wheel that spun around for eternity!"

"Or about Oedipus, who poked his own eyes out!" Hades smiled at the memory. "That's a great story!"

"No," said Iris, "that's not what I meant at all. I meant a

143

story that might teach them something, not just scare them—a story about love and adventure, something inspiring."

Hades looked confused; Persephone looked thoughtful.

"Well, I'm not sure we know any stories like that," said Hades.

"Yes we do," said Persephone, and she began.

Chapter 22

When I was a girl, we had only perfect days. Winter was un-heard of, and rain fell in the nicest, warmest way, so that you could run barefoot through it. All the nymphs of the meadows were my friends, because I was daughter of the mighty Deme-ter, goddess of the harvest. They called me simply "Kore," the maiden. When I stepped on the ground, daisies sprang up from my right foot and black-eyed Susans from my left.

On the day my girlhood ended, I was gathering lilies for a garland. I saw a blue flower shot through with orange. It was perfect. I knelt down and reached for it, and as I touched the stem, everything went black. The smell of fire and rot filled the air. There was a terrible tightness around my right ankle, like a thick iron shackle. That was my husband's hand.

I was terrified. I dropped my hem, and my last thought as he took me to hell was that I had let all the flowers fall.

I only dimly remember the ride there. His horses were un-godly beasts with fire for breath and glowing embers for eyes. We traveled through amazing places—caverns full of topaz and amethyst; magnificent sunken oceans; underground trees with silver leaves—and yet they seemed dark and horrible to my eyes, all those sun-starved wonders.

The chariot shook from the demon horses' speed. Hades had to hold me down or I would have fallen and perished. It was the first time a man had ever dared to touch me. Wherever he set his hands, I felt as if my skin were stained. That was an awful time, the first ride into hell. The whole time we traveled, Hades stayed silent, just looking at me with those deep, gray eyes of his: the eyes of the dead.

When we arrived at his palace, he finally spoke. "You will be happy here with me. I love you so much. Beautiful Persephone."

"I will never, never be happy here," I told him, "for you have cruelly taken me from my friends and my mother and my beautiful Earth. I will never be happy here in your ugly, sun-less world, and I will not suffer you to touch me with your hands, which stink of death."

With that I turned my back on him and walked off on my own. I did not know where I was going. I just wanted to get away. But the world of the dead is a frightening place, Iris. It is everywhere the same: grim and gray and cold. I walked and walked, crying and tearing at my clothes. I called out to my mother, Demeter, to my father, Zeus, to all my nymph friends. When my feet touched the ground, no flowers sprang up. The shades of the dead whispered and pointed at me as I walked by. I began to tire and to shiver. I stood for a while and stared at Sisyphus, the king who had been cursed to roll a boulder up a hill for eternity. Whenever he got to the top, it slipped and rolled back down. What despair! And no end to it, ever. My legs failed me and I sank to the ground. All I saw in every direction was vast gray expanse. Let me die here, I thought, and though immortal, I dearly wished to die on that day. Then I heard a buzzing sound in my ear.

"Does my lady wish to return now?" said a kind female voice. It was a moth, a silvery white one with fuzzy antennae.

"Who are you?" I asked.

"I am my lady's servant, sent by Hades to follow you and take you back home when you tire." The moth settled on my arm, tickling my skin with her tiny legs.

"What is your name?"

"Lucifer. But you can call me Lucy."

"Lucy, I am afraid that I am too tired to walk back to the castle. I must rest for a while. Then you can show me which way it is."

"But my lady does not understand the ways of hell," she said, laughing. "You are in the land of Hades and you are his beloved. When you want to go to the castle, you need only speak his name and it will appear."

"Lucy, I will not speak it. His name is poison on my lips."

She sighed. I shivered and clutched my tunic as the winds howled around me. Lucy fluttered around, talking to the shades. I let my eyes close, then curled myself up into a little ball. Lucy sat on my ear and murmured, "My lady is very proud, my beautiful lady." And then I slept. Her words echoed through my dreams. They seemed to be spoken again and again, and the voice changed and grew deeper. "My beautiful Persephone." Now it was Hades' voice, and in my fatigue-soaked dreams (for I had given myself a fever) I was aware of his lifting me up and carrying me into his palace. He laid me down on a white marble bed, while Lucy fluttered around muttering, "Very proud, very proud." And I remember feeling happy that I had not called his name.

I lay ill with fever for a long time. I don't know how long. A nurse tended to me, Lucy sat on my coverlet, and Hades brooded over me. When I did not improve, the centaur Chiron was sent for. The famous healer came to my bedside and peeked under my fevered eyelids so kindly.

"Little Kore," he said, "smell this." He held under my nose a single white rose, fresh-plucked. The fragrance of that flower woke me from my fevered sleep. He smiled when he saw that it had worked, then said to me, "Like cures like."

When I awoke, pulled up to consciousness by the clean, sweet smell of rose, I thought for a moment the whole abduction had been a terrible dream and that I was still safe on the earth's warm surface. But I saw there was something gray and sickly about the light. And there was no smell of earth. Then I looked over Chiron's shoulder and saw the anxious gaze of my husband, watching to see if I was healed. My stomach sank as I realized the awful dream was true. I turned my back to them all and curled up, crying.

"Can you cure this sadness of hers, Chiron?" I heard Hades

ask in his deep toneless voice. "I dearly wish her heart to be at ease."

Chiron snorted. "Sire, that is beyond my power. He who makes the wound of love must heal it himself."

"If you want my heart to be easy, then return me to my home," I cried. "Let me ride there on Chiron's back. Ah, Chiron"—I turned to him—"if you bring me back to my mother, she will cover you with the gemstones of the earth. All your fields will bear fat yields of grain, and any nymph of the forest or field shall be your bride, anyone you desire. Please, Chiron, take me home."

I think Chiron might have done it. But Hades' voice cut into my reverie.

"That cannot be," he said, and Chiron lowered his eyes. I hated my husband then.

Time passed slowly. I could not measure its pace, for in the underworld there is neither sunrise nor sunset. Hades left me alone mostly, though each evening he would summon me to dinner, where we sat facing each other across a long stone table. He wore heavy velvet robes, worked through with golden thread, and a ruby-encrusted crown. But the finery only made him look like the corpse of a king, arrayed at a state funeral. He ate, and I watched. Though Hades offered me the finest delicacies, I never parted my lips, but sat stone-faced and silent. I would not take food from his table.

One night Hades said to me, "I must go to Mount Olympus tomorrow. My brother Zeus has summoned me. I will be gone for a week."

"I want to go, too. I want to see Demeter."

"I know you want to go. You remind me of that fact constantly." It was the first time he had ever snapped at me. "But you will remain here. Be contented, Persephone; you will be free from the burden of my hateful presence for a full week. I will see you upon my return." He got up and strode out of the hall, banging the door shut behind him. I felt strangely embarrassed.

While Hades was gone, the days seemed even longer. I was terribly bored. After my illness, I no longer wanted to wander alone through the wilderness of the dead. I took to roaming the castle with Lucy at my side. She gave me details about each room since she had been Hades' servant for thousands of years. She always snuck in bits of praise for her master, in hopes that my heart would open to him.

"This is the queen's suite. My lord built it especially for you when he saw you. See how the walls are inlaid with ivory flowers and leaves of silver? 'No artifice can match her beauty,' he told the builders, 'yet make it set with flowers as befits the maiden of spring.'"

"I prefer real flowers, Lucy," I said, though I was secretly pleased at the praise. Hades never told me he had made the rooms just for me.

"Well, if you prefer real flowers, then you must visit the castle garden."

"The garden!" I was shocked. "There is a garden in hell?"

So she took me. After so many weeks of the gloom of dead things, the gardens of Hades' palace made me drunk with pleasure. I wandered among the rows and spoke to each blossom, the way I used to do at home. But these flowers were different from Chiron's white rose. They had no fragrance. They were cold and perfect, as if made of wax.

"Ah, my lady visits the gardens at last."

A slight man appeared out of the shrubbery. He bowed to me, his small eyes glittering.

"Permit me the honor of introducing myself. I am the gardener. My name is Ascalaphus. Welcome."

He gave me a tour of his garden, pointing out plants that I knew and plants that I had never seen. Yet always they were cold to the touch and without fragrance. Ascalaphus's glittery eyes caught everything, and he noticed how I bent to sniff each one.

"Ah, perhaps the princess wishes her nostrils to be as delighted as her eyes. Such a dainty nose she has, too." He reached out a blade of grass and traced it over the profile of my nose. I pulled back in shock, and Lucy flew angrily into his face.

"You forget yourself, gardener," I said.

"My humble apologies, Princess," he said, chuckling. "I work with these fake flowers all day. Seldom do I see a real one." He bowed until his head touched the ground. "But if my lady wishes to smell something sweet, she should follow me. This is the only thing in the garden with real fragrance."

In the very center of Hades' garden stood a tree whose branches were heavy with fruit. Ascalaphus took me there.

"Smell this."

I lifted to my nose the firm red pomegranate he offered. Amazingly, it had fragrance. I smelled it again and again, filling my nose with the syrupy-sweet smell of autumn orchards.

I broke it open and smelled the inside, delighting at the sight of the little jewel-like seeds spilling into my palms. Suddenly I felt terribly hungry. It had been over a month since I had eaten, and the seeds tempted me. I lifted one to my lips.

"Yes, my lady, eat the fruit. It is very sweet."

What would it matter if I ate one, *I thought,* just one. *Hades would never know. I slipped a tiny red seed into my mouth and bit through the crisp skin. It was delicious, hauntingly sweet and tart, but it was gone so quickly. I ate five more seeds, one after the other. They exploded like sweet fireworks in my mouth.*

I looked up and saw Ascalaphus watching me. Lucy was flying around very fast in tight little circles. The gardener whispered something to her and smiled.

"Have more, Persephone," said Lucy, but I would not. Something about the way the gardener smiled made me nervous.

"Let's go see more of the castle, Lucy." And we hurried off.

The next day, my husband returned. To my great delight, he was not alone but had brought with him my cousin, fleet-footed Hermes. I had never noticed before how young Hermes looked, but my time in hell had aged me. I ran to embrace him and ask for news of my mother and all our family on Mount Olympus.

"Your mother is not well since you left us," said the boy, with unusual gravity. "She is bereft. She tears out her hair and cries and will not tend to the earth. She says that without her beloved daughter, there is no comfort for her under the sun and no work that interests her. Everywhere on Earth there is

famine and death. It is horrible, cousin. The mortals starve, unable to make the frozen earth yield a single sheaf of wheat. The animals die with nothing to feed on. Dionysus mourns his beautiful vineyards, where the grapes lie frozen and shriveled on the callous earth. Apollo and Artemis, the lovely twins of day and night, cry as they drive their chariots across the sky and look down on such suffering. Even Ares complains, for the mortals have no strength to wage war. We all beg your mother to relent, but in vain. She says that the earth will lie frozen and sterile until you return, and so Zeus sends me to fetch you and bring you back to her."

I clapped my hands in joy. My mother had won! I would go back to her, and everything would be as it had been.

"There is only one question I need to ask you, cousin Persephone. Have you eaten any food here? The Fates decree that anyone who eats the food of the underworld must remain there forever."

"She has taken no food, Hermes," said my husband, who had been listening to my cousin's speech with a bowed head. "I know it well, for we dine together every night, and she looks on the food and on me with the same cold scorn. Take her back to her mother and I wish her joy there. It is clear that she has none here."

For a moment I felt sorry for my husband, but then my thoughts were overwhelmed by giddy happiness. To be free again! To smell the fresh air!

"Excuse me, sir," said a nasal voice that made my stomach sink. It was Ascalaphus, who had waited for his moment. "The girl has indeed eaten here. I saw it."

"When?" asked Hades excitedly.

"When you were gone, Master. She came to the garden with Lucifer and ate my fruit." I saw the traitorous moth, perched on his shoulder.

"Yes, it's true, yes, yes," Lucy repeated.

"But," I said, tears running down my cheeks, "only six pomegranate seeds. Surely, Hermes, that can't count. I just wanted to taste them." Hermes looked uncertain. Hades beamed.

"She has eaten! Ah, my beautiful Persephone, now you must stay with me. I am glad, so glad, that you ate that fruit. I will serve you platters of fruit, perfect fruit of every color and flavor. You will stay with me and be happy, and we will rule this kingdom together."

"I will never be happy here. I want to go home. Please, Hermes, take me home." I got down on my knees and begged, but Hermes would not take me. When I cried and tore my hair, he said that since I had eaten so little, perhaps Zeus could make an exception. He promised to return with news.

But I was in a frenzy of despair. To have been so close to rescue and have it taken away again was more than I could bear. I could not stand to wait and see what Zeus would rule, but decided I would escape. In my desperation I conceived a foolish plan.

Five rivers run through hell. The first is the river Styx, upon which the gods swear their oaths. The Styx was too well guarded, and its waters were fierce and bitter. I could not swim the Acheron because of Charon, who ferried the dead souls across it. All Charon cared about was gold, and he would be sure to catch me and turn me in to Hades for a reward. I could not swim the Cocytus, the river of lamentation, because I could not bear to hear the wailing of the dead souls who clustered around its banks. And I could not cross the Phlegethon, of course, for it flowed with liquid fire. So I settled on the rash plan of swimming the Lethe, the river of oblivion, whose waters are sweet and gentle. But I did not understand the true nature of that water; no maelstrom could do as much damage as the Lethe with its deathly calm.

I stole out of my room while my husband and Lucy slept. I still loved the moth, despite her betrayal. She genuinely cared for both Hades and for me, and she had been my only friend in hell. I bade her a silent farewell. I brought nothing with me, for there was nothing in Hades' palace that mattered to me, except for Chiron's white rose, which I had kept alive in a crystal vase. I fastened it to my dress and ran to the Lethe's bank.

The fragrance rising off the water was dizzying: thick, sickly sweet, like incense. When I inhaled it, my eyelids fluttered and I nearly slept. Then a fresh breeze came and I jerked back into wakefulness. For an instant I could not remember why I was there. Then it came back to me: I was escaping. You would think this brief bout of forgetfulness would have warned me, but it did not. Perhaps my judgment was already addled by the Lethe's power.

With a quick prayer—"Mother Demeter, be with me"—I tied up my skirt and dived in. I expected the cold jolt of river water, but the Lethe was warm as a fresh-drawn bath. My mouth opened in surprise and the Lethe filled it. I learned *what all dead souls know, that forgetfulness tastes like honey and wine and warm milk. The water tasted better than the nectar we drink to stay immortal. I swallowed again and again. In my madness, I wanted to smell it, too, and so I inhaled, filling my lungs with the water.*

When I started to drown, I remembered something. I remembered that I was supposed to be swimming toward the far shore. But I couldn't remember how to swim. My limbs felt numb and heavy. A moment later, I couldn't remember what swimming was. Oh well, *I thought,* it can't have been that important.

I closed my eyes and began to die. Yes, Iris, there are ways that even immortals can die, and I had found one of them. But the part of me that loved life woke up the rest of me. My eyes snapped open, and terror filled me. I remembered nothing. I only knew that I was dying and needed help. I windmilled my arms, but my strength was gone. Chiron's rose came loose from my bodice and the water filled with petals.

Terrified, I searched my brain for a clue to what was happening. Who was I? Where was I? I watched one of the white petals from Chiron's rose drift this way and that. It reminded me of something, the way it fluttered. My thoughts started to drift the way they do right before sleep. I remembered that there was a white moth who used to flutter like that. She was my friend. She had told me—darkness and warmth started to creep over me—she had told me about a castle. I closed my eyes and smiled. There was a magic castle that would come to me whenever I called out for its king. The poor king. He was very sad because his queen had gone away. The king's name was . . .

"Hades," I whispered, and died.

They say that when the bubble that contained Hades' name broke to the surface of the Lethe, all the shades in hell heard me screaming for my love. They say that even Charon set down his staff and wept for me.

But Hades was already riverside. The moment the bubble broke, he was there, pulling my body out of that water that even he, its lord, had to struggle against. But he was very strong and got me out quickly. It was only the second time he had held me in his arms. And this time, as he kissed life back into my lips, I rewarded him with a smile.

"Hades," I said again. "The poor king." My mind was blank. All I knew was that a sad handsome man was staring at me with worry. Why is he so sad? I thought. I put my hand in his, to comfort him.

"Ah, Persephone, I feared for you greatly. My love. Do you—do you willingly take my hand?" He looked down with disbelief at my small hand in his. When I heard my name, it all came back to me: my childhood, my abduction, my desperate plan to escape, and Hades' rescue of me. I looked at our joined hands and sighed.

"I suppose I do."

"My love, you will not regret this." He squeezed my hand. "It's not so bad here, Persephone, you'll see. I know it is not what you would have chosen, but my land is vast and full of wonders, and I lay it at your feet. Here in hell, I rival Zeus in his power, and you will be my queen, the powerful Queen of the Underworld. That is not such a bad thing to be."

I smiled sadly at my husband, for I knew that it is not always given to us to choose our path in life. Sometimes the path chooses us.

When Hermes returned to report my father's ruling, he found me seated calmly at Hades' side, in my own throne of ruby. Zeus had agreed to a compromise. Since I had eaten only six pomegranate seeds, he decreed, I would spend six months of the year in the underworld as Hades' bride; I would return to Earth to spend the remaining six with my mother. Zeus is a wise mediator.

While I was underground, my mother grieved and neglected her duties, and so on Earth it was autumn and winter. When I returned to her, she rejoiced and hung the trees with spring flowers and summer fruit. And so the seasons were born.

Chapter 23

Iris found it hard to resurface from the world of Persephone's story, which had been so beautiful and so sad.

"Thank you for the story, Persephone."

"Don't mention it," said Persephone. "Really don't mention it. To Zeus. We'll get in big trouble."

Hades nodded and handed Iris another doughnut. "In fact, why don't you take the rest of the day off. As a little show of our good faith."

Iris thought she could get used to this, having the principal in her debt. She skipped out into the sunshine and headed for the strip mall, where Athena and Artemis had their office. This had come as a big surprise to Iris, for she had never noticed the office before. But the gods seemed to have ways to evade unwanted attention. Her mother would say they were good at camouflage.

Iris's backpack flopped up and down. Her sneakers beat out an impatient rhythm on the sidewalk. She felt like she couldn't get there fast enough.

Someone had been watching over her, the way gods watched over heroes in myths, providing aid and advice. That someone had sent her *Bulfinch's Mythology* in the mail, had sent her the rainbow shawl. And the more she thought it over, the more that someone had to be Athena. After all, Athena's symbol was the owl, and Athena was the goddess of weaving, so she'd be able to weave a rainbow if anyone could. She was also the goddess of wisdom, and the note in the book had said KNOWLEDGE IS POWER.

But why me? Of all the people Athena could choose to watch over, why would it be me? Iris jogged around the curve of asphalt that stretched from the Monster Burger drive-in to the strip of storefronts. *There's nothing special about me.* There were dozens of kids at her school who were more likely heroines. They got better grades, or were cute or rich or good at sports, or winners of violin prizes or spelling bees. Iris was none of these things.

But secretly she *did* feel special. She always had. She was just special in a way that school couldn't measure, but maybe Athena could.

Iris stopped outside the office door, her heart pounding from the run. She understood now why she had never noticed the office before. The door and window were completely covered with brown paper. Only a hand-lettered sign taped to the outside of the door indicated that it was not vacant. The sign read DOUBLE-A INVESTIGATION. BY AP-POINTMENT ONLY.

Iris tried the door, but it was locked, so she knocked on the glass.

"Who's there?" a woman's voice barked.

"My name is Iris."

"Who sent you?"

"Ares."

The door swung open, and an owl flew in Iris's face. Iris put up her hands to protect herself and staggered back-ward. When the bird had gone, Iris was left staring at the point of a silver arrow. The woman holding the bow had to be Artemis, because she had her twin brother Apollo's face, only darker skinned and more feminine. Artemis wore her hair in long braids held back by a silver circlet, and her clothes were the kind a hunter wears.

"Just a precaution, miss," Artemis said, as a second woman emerged from the store, caught the owl on her wrist, and frisked Iris for weapons.

Athena was Asian, with short-cropped black hair and startling gray eyes. She was dressed like a martial artist, in a silken *gi,* with a long, curved sword at her side. Athena's hands were deft, and Iris knew that if she had hidden a single razor blade in her pocket, Athena would have caught it.

"She's clean," Athena said, and she winked at Iris. Artemis put down her bow.

Their office was spartan and smelled of cinnamon in-cense. Two desks sat against the walls, with a perch between them for the owl and a chair for a client. Various spears, arrows, and pieces of armor were stacked in one corner. The walls were bare, except for a large poster of the moon. Athena gestured to the chair.

"Coffee, Iris?"

"No, thank you."

"Whiskey?"

"No, thank you. It's, um, it's really an honor to meet you both. And thank you for the gifts, Athena. They were from you, weren't they?"

Athena held up her hand for silence. "Business first, Iris. Always business first. Let's hear about this Tofu-licious outfit." She flipped on a tape recorder.

Iris told her about her mother losing her job, and then about the Sibyl's prophecy and how that gave Iris the idea to sue. She said Ares wanted to look into the company, find out anything about them that might help the case.

"Say no more," said Artemis. "This kind of corporation usually has more skeletons in its closet than Zeus has girlfriends. Should be easy: a few moonlit vigils."

"A few visits from the wide-eyed owl," said Athena.

"A few trees enlisted to eavesdrop," said Artemis.

"A few long-range photos and tapped phone lines," said Athena. "Tofu's a soft business. Probably won't even need to rough anyone up."

"Still, gotta be careful, Sister. The enemy's the enemy."

"You know me, Sister. I make carelessness my enemy."

Iris sat and watched them talk. There was something strong and pure about the two of them that filled her with admiration. They were both very beautiful, but the style of their beauty was different from Aphrodite's and Amphitrite's. Athena and Artemis were boyish, that was the only word Iris could think of. Yet they were too beautiful to be boys.

"They call you . . ."—Iris hesitated, not wanting to be rude—"they call you the virgin goddesses."

"Yep, that's us," said Artemis. "Not to say that we haven't slipped from time to time. There was once a hunter named Orion, perhaps you've seen him in the sky?" Iris nodded. "He was very handsome. But I shot him. Accidentally. That was the last time I was tempted."

"We've got too much else to do," said Athena. "For a warrior, love is a distraction. It breaks the stillness of her mind."

Artemis added, "It gets a hunter off her scent, dulls her reflexes, weakens her legs."

"Wow," said Iris, "I'd like to be a warrior, too. And stay unmarried, like the two of you."

But Athena looked Iris in the eyes and shook her head. "You say that now, but it is not your path. You are young, and you will change. Remember that love is a goddess, too. And a gentler goddess than us."

Iris shivered. Athena's bright gray eyes were almost frightening. "I don't want to change."

"Yet, you will, Iris. This is the way things are."

"Athena, you know so much. I didn't just come here to ask about the case. It was you who sent me the gifts, wasn't it?"

"Yes."

Iris smiled. "Thank you. I love them. But I wondered why you chose me to give those things to." She was scared to ask Athena the real question she had in her mind, because it meant so much to her. With all her heart, she wanted the answer to be *yes*.

But Athena shook her head. "The answer to that question is *no*, Iris."

Iris hung her head, ashamed that she had even thought it. "I'm not a goddess, then?" she whispered, unable to control the tears running down her face. "I'm not immortal?" She had so hoped. She had hoped that Athena had chosen her to be the new messenger goddess.

"No." Athena smiled bitterly. "Do you really want that, little one, after what you have seen of us?"

Artemis said, "You think you want it, but you do not. Look at us, Iris, lingering past the time when our powers were full. We wane and wane. Now we are like the moon in its tiniest sliver."

"Ah, but the moon always waxes again, Sister," said Athena, "and we never will."

"True," said Artemis, and she reached out for Athena's hand. "We will continue to fade until nothing is left of us but the poems and the statues and the old stories."

Iris couldn't stop the tears now, but she didn't know if she was crying for herself or for the goddesses.

"Ah, Iris. This is the way things are." Athena reached out for Iris's hand, and Artemis took the other, so that they stood in a circle: the two grown women and the small girl.

Iris felt electricity flow through their joined hands. As she looked at the goddesses, it seemed to her that Artemis was naked and shone like the moon. Athena was covered in gleaming armor with a plumed helmet hiding her face. When Athena spoke again, her voice was the one warriors had heard on ancient battlefields, urging them on to glory.

"That's why it is important for you to know these stories, Iris. As long as they are alive, *we* are alive, too.

"Yes, there is a reason that I sent those gifts to you, Iris, as opposed to anyone else. Still, you may not like the reason. There is a Buddhist saying that the truth is like a dog confronted by a bowl of burning grease: He cannot walk away because it is too delicious, but he cannot lick it because it burns. The truth calls to you, Iris, but it may also hurt you. Still, I wanted you to *know*. I wanted you to know *who you really are*."

And Athena told Iris a story.

Chapter 24

You admire us now, Iris, but my sister and I are nothing compared with what we were. In the height of my power, whole armies lived and died by a wave of my spear. I was the goddess of war and wisdom, also the goddess of the great art of weaving. I was a virgin goddess, pure and fierce. You can't imagine such power.

As Athena spoke, she seemed to grow larger and larger. Iris tilted back her head and shaded her eyes with one hand. It was as if she were standing at the base of the Statue of Liberty, looking up. Athena gleamed with gold and gray armor. Far up in the sky, her gray eyes blazed beneath a plumed helmet. One hand held a spear; the other carried a shield that had the head of a snake-haired woman on it. A huge owl swooped down from above and landed on Athena's shoulder with a screech so loud that Iris let go of the goddesses' hands, dropped to her knees, and covered her ears with her hands.

Then Athena took off her helmet. She seemed to deflate, and the armor and weapons faded away. The owl was back to its normal size, and Athena looked very small and human again.

"Do not fear, Iris. Those days are over for me. There was a time, however, when insulting Pallas Athena was no small thing."

Rumors started reaching me on Mount Olympus of a mortal girl named Arachne, whose skill in weaving was unparalleled. They said her colors had the shine of a flower's petals and the clarity of a butterfly's wings. They said the figures she wove seemed ready to speak, laugh, and jump right out of the fabric. They said there was truth in her work—that it told the past and the present and that she was practicing to weave the future.

This much was fine. The girl was ambitious and skilled, and I wished her well, although the project of weaving the future was obviously impossible. But then the rumors took a different turn. They said that the girl's work was being compared to mine. Imagine that! People were telling her it was almost as fine as what came off gray-eyed Athena's loom, and asked her if she had been taught to weave by the goddess herself.

The girl was said to have replied: "I stand in no one's shadow, but in the light of my own truth. Only in this light should you view my work. I taught myself to weave and weaving is all I do. I do it better than anyone, mortal or im-mortal. If Athena herself were here before me, I would say as much to her."

I was infuriated, and decided to pay the girl a visit.

Arachne's story was well-known. At age four, she had started playing with her mother's loom and shuttle. At five, she was the youngest-ever champion at the All-Athens Weave-Off. By six, she was selling her own clothing line.

I knocked on her door in the guise of a stooped old woman: "Yarn for sale! Fine yarn of all colors for the famous weaver Arachne! Come see! Come buy!" She yelled at me to go away, and told me that she spun all her own yarn.

"But," I said, "at least open the door and look at what I have. You might be surprised. I have one skein made from Jason's Golden Fleece: very, very rare. It is soft as silk, strong as iron, and it shines like sunlight falling on the sea."

"From the Golden Fleece? It can't be authentic." She opened the door just wide enough to stick out her hand. I put the skein in her palm, and she withdrew the hand and shut the door. There was a moment of silence and then the door opened fully. Arachne stood there with the wool in her hands. She was surprisingly small, with the stooped posture and muscled shoulders of one who spends all day at the loom. Her dark eyes were filled with tears as she gazed at the wool.

"This is so flawless," she said, "it is very moving." My heart opened to her then. Only a true artist could cry over a skein of yarn.

"Yes," I said, "I know what you mean."

"How beautiful it would be as trim for a white linen robe,

168

or as a mantle." There was wonder in Arachne's voice, and I suddenly realized she couldn't be more than sixteen years old.

"I used the other skein to make a bridal veil," I said, thinking of the glorious piece I had made as a wedding present to Hebe, the goddess of youth, when she married Hercules. "The bride had golden hair and was of surpassing beauty."

"That sounds lovely," said Arachne. "What design did you use? I just completed a bridal veil for the queen of Ethiopia; would you like to see it?" She turned and entered the house. "Come in! See, what I did was I invented a process to create a scalloped hem, like a seashell. I could teach you if you want to learn it."

And before I knew it, I was discussing technique with Arachne like we were two old friends. It was easy to see that she was desperate for someone to talk to. She talked about dyeing and spinning; she talked about what patterns to use; she talked about what to feed the sheep to make their wool grow faster. To tell you the truth, she astounded me with her knowledge of the craft. I asked her about the rumors I had heard that she was trying to divine the future with her art. She looked embarrassed for a moment.

"I do not often speak of this, because no one understands me. The truth is, Grandmother, I am very ambitious. Right now, you will find in my weavings the stories of the past and the images of the present, but I am not satisfied. I want to weave the future as well.

"You see, when I am not weaving, my mind is like an empty house filled with dust. But weaving opens all my windows wide, so the birdsong comes in. I get these flashes when I

169

weave, flashes about things that are going to happen or things that have happened.

"But right now, these flashes scare me or confuse me, because I am not good enough at weaving to know how to put them in the cloth. If I could just get my left hand to move a little faster . . . And I haven't found a way to capture the grayness of things at dusk. You know how at a certain point near sunset it gets so dark that it's hard to tell the difference between colors? I want to be able to weave that.

"I think if I keep practicing every day, I can teach myself how to do these and many more things. And then a time will come, perhaps when I am around fifty, when there won't be a single thing I can't do at the loom, and then I will relax and let the birdsong come out. And then, my art will tell the future."

I smiled—she had won my heart—and prepared to leave. She stopped me.

"And what can I pay you for the golden yarn? I can call my mother to bring some money. It is exquisite; I will pay any price you ask."

"It is yours, Arachne, with my compliments."

"No, Grandmother, I cannot accept such a gift. My work has made me a rich woman. You must allow me to pay you."

"I will accept no payment from you. Please, take it as my gift. From one artist to another."

She bowed low. "I am in your debt."

I wish I had left right then and let the girl be! But for some reason, I needed to throw my weight around. I added, "You are second to none on Earth, but only to our divine patroness Athena."

She snorted and said, "Athena! Everyone always throws that name at me like I am supposed to be impressed. Take my word for it, Grandmother; Athena could learn a few things from me, and from you as well. We are too much in awe of the gods."

"Be careful, girl," I said, "you must know your place."

"My place is first," she said. "I can't stand being second to anyone, not even a goddess."

I felt the anger start to rise in me. "It is no shame to acknowledge the superiority of those greater than us. Athena is a wise, powerful goddess, the patroness and inventor of the art you love so much. You should beg her forgiveness and ask her blessing on your work."

"What do I need her forgiveness for? For being a better artist than her?"

"You are not a better artist than her."

"How do you know? How does anyone know? You know, I don't even think Athena really exists. And if she does exist, and if she were here in front of me, I would challenge her to a contest at the loom. No magic or tricks, just her skills against mine."

I felt my disguise start to fade as my anger rose. My old woman's face began to firm up. The white hair turned to gray; the gray hair turned to black. My transformation was lost on Arachne, though, who was so full of emotion that she did not see what was right before her.

"Beware, child. You are playing with fire." My voice had changed, too, growing deep and resonant. "I will give you one more chance: Beg Athena's pardon. Get down on your knees and—"

"Never! I could never get on my knees before anyone. But, why are you so worried about Athena?" Arachne looked at me in confusion, her face white with shock. She shielded her eyes as a halo blazed around me. My voice rang out loud enough to reach the neighboring houses:

"FOOLISH GIRL, I GRANT YOU YOUR WISH, THOUGH IT WILL BE YOUR LAST! ATHENA CONSENTS TO A CONTEST AT THE LOOM. YOU WILL SEE MY SKILL AND IT WILL PUT YOURS TO SHAME. AND AFTER YOU HAVE BEEN DE-FEATED, YOU WILL INDEED KNEEL BEFORE ME AND BEG FOR YOUR LIFE! AND PERHAPS I WILL SPARE IT."

The words were like thunder, and the poor girl shook with fear. Yet she stood up very straight, squared her stooped shoulders, and looked into my eyes.

"So be it, Athena. You may find that victory is not as sure as you think. While you have been in heaven drinking nectar, I have been practicing my craft." Strange to say, the girl's words sent a shiver of fear through me, and this made me even angrier.

"WE WILL BEGIN AT ONCE!" I yelled. "THE NYMPHS SHALL JUDGE." A large crowd of both nymphs and mortals had already gathered, drawn by my voice.

"The nymphs will not judge fairly," Arachne said. Tears were flowing down her cheeks. "You are immortal, and they will be afraid to anger you."

"Then they are far wiser than you," I said. "Enough delays. Set up your loom."

To give the girl credit, she wasted no time. We set up our

172

looms facing each other across a large sunny clearing just downhill from Arachne's house. The crowd of spectators began to place bets on the winner. I saw my half brother Hermes, who was always where the action was, circulating through the crowd, disguised as a bookie. He set the odds at four-to-one in my favor.

The afternoon was very hot, and so we took off our mantles and worked bare-armed in the sun. The crowd murmured at the beauty of our arms as they rose and fell in quick rhythm, the lean muscles gleaming with sweat.

I chose a theme for my work that would put Arachne in her place: The Naming of Athens. It was the story of my greatest triumph, my claiming of Athens as a patron city. In the tapestry, I stood before the people of Athens, looking majestic, gesturing to a young olive tree with one hand. The Athenians clustered around my tree, and their faces were filled with marvel and joy.

I wove a border of olive branches around the whole scene. This was a sign of my power, but also of peace. I meant this as a message to Arachne, that she could still seek peace if she wished, for weaving always soothes me, and my anger had cooled toward her. I had indeed produced a masterwork that day—The Naming of Athens was my finest piece ever, and I believed that no mortal could produce anything approaching its beauty.

Lifting my eyes from my work took effort, like waking from an engrossing dream. I saw that Arachne, too, had finished a large piece. I recognized in her face the same feeling of deep contentment that I felt. She was happy with her work. We held each other's gaze for a long moment.

On a sudden impulse, I reached down for my boxwood shuttle. I gripped it so strongly that the wood almost cracked in two.

Arachne and I stood up at the same time. I threw back my sore shoulders, and she stretched her neck. We nodded to each other grimly as we switched places at the looms. I heard her whistle in appreciation as she stood before my work. I faced hers and gasped.

Arachne had completely abandoned the traditional way of weaving, which placed one scene in the center and a few little scenes as border motifs. Instead, her tapestry had little scenes everywhere, the tiny figures so detailed and lifelike that it seemed they would wriggle right up out of the fabric. The effect was overwhelming. It was like looking down at the world from high above. For a moment, I was filled with love for this mortal girl. I was so moved by what she had created that I felt ready to forgive everything. And then I realized her theme.

Every little scene involved some incident of embarrassment to the gods: all the times Zeus had been caught by Hera flirting with mortal girls, all the times Apollo had chased after nymphs, all the times we had quarreled, erred, or been defeated. I felt embarrassed to see these images, and my anger at the girl returned with fuller force. How dare she?

But there were three things in Arachne's tapestry that puzzled me.

Right in the center of the scenes was an image of me as I looked at that very moment, looking at a miniature image of Arachne's tapestry. The miniature tapestry that the woven Athena faced was an exact copy of the real one, and it even con-

tained a smaller Athena looking at a tinier tapestry. This continued for about six Athenas, until they got so small that you couldn't see them. In all of these pictures, I had a very ugly, jealous expression on my face, and I held a bloody shuttle in my hand. But why? Why was my shuttle bloody?

Secondly, there was a woman depicted among the lovers of Zeus who was unfamiliar to me. How could Arachne know of an affair that I was ignorant of?

Thirdly, Arachne's whole weaving was bordered with an intricate, weblike design, and a tiny black eight-legged creature sat in the lower right corner, just above Arachne's signature. What could the strange creature be?

Before I knew what I was doing, I pivoted around to face Arachne where she stood trembling in front of my tapestry, and struck her hard across the face with the shuttle. "ARROGANT GIRL. HOW DARE YOU?" She screamed. I struck her four times like that, until my shuttle dripped with blood. I looked down at the shuttle, amazed. How had she known?

"She has succeeded in her highest aim: telling the future," said a calm voice behind me. I turned around and saw Apollo sitting cross-legged on a stone, tuning his lute. "Her work predicts events far off in the future, and even her own doom. As you and I know, Sister, it is a lonely business being an artist."

"What are you saying, Phoebus?"

"I am saying you should spare her."

"Spare her? How can I spare her after she has insulted us all so deeply?" But I knew in my heart that Apollo was right, for I was the goddess of wisdom and peace as well as the goddess of war and craft, and I felt my anger fading away once again.

175

"You have already punished her enough, Athena. She is shamed and her face is ruined for life." I knew he was right.

Arachne seemed to have disappeared. I ran up the hill to her cottage. All my respect for the girl came back. I remembered how we had spent the day together and how happy she had been to have someone to talk to. Apollo was right; making art is a lonely business. I would befriend the girl. We could weave together once in a while and teach each other new things.

I pulled open her door.

"Arachne?"

There was no answer, although I thought I saw some movement in the darkness. I had a horrible feeling in the pit of my stomach. Something about that movement terrified me. I yelled out her name again, louder this time, and pulled aside the shutters. It was dusk, and things had lost their color.

In the gray light, I saw her body swing. I wept. She had used a stack of her own tapestries to reach the rafters and the golden yarn for a noose. There was nothing I could do. I lacked the power to bring back a human life. But I could alter life's form, so I took the tears from my cheeks and sprinkled them on her hanging form. She shrank and darkened, wriggling on her thread.

"Ah, poor Arachne. Why were you so stubborn? I would have forgiven you. But all I can do now is to make your weaving immortal. You will be the mother of a race of weavers.

"I give you this gift, that your craftsmanship will be one of the great mysteries of nature. Children will marvel at your intricate offerings—at how they catch the dew and the sunlight.

You *will* hang from your gleaming thread wherever high rafters are found."

And as I changed her into the first-ever spider, I thought with a start of the way she had bordered her tapestry with a web and of the little creature she had woven in the lower-right corner. Arachne had known. She had known all along how her story would end.

Chapter 25

"That was a great story, Athena, but it didn't have anything to do with me."

Athena smiled. "Oh no?"

Iris looked from her to Artemis, baffled. "Well, I don't think it did. Did I miss something?"

"Anything worth finding is worth hunting," said Artemis.

"Zeus is in the details," said Athena, her gray eyes laughing. "Time for you to go now, Iris. We've got some detecting to do, and so do you."

Iris walked home so she could think things over. She retold herself the story of Arachne, starting at the beginning and going all the way through, but she couldn't understand what part of it had to do with her.

The walk took her alongside the turnpike, and the cars *whoosh*ed past, sending her hair flying up around her ears. Iris liked it up on the turnpike overpass. The sound barriers loomed beside her like castle walls, beyond which she could see the whole town. She saw the playing fields and blacktops of Erebus, where she imagined Persephone and Hades sitting in their office, talking about the changes she had suggested. She saw the strip mall, where Athena and Artemis would be plotting their stakeout of Tofu-licious. All around were streets full of boxy Middleville houses, and green patches of Pennsylvania forest. Iris shaded her eyes with her hand and picked out among them the apartment complex where she lived.

Iris was disappointed that she wasn't a goddess, but she supposed she couldn't have everything. Being a friend of gods and goddesses was almost as cool as being one. Athena and Artemis had left a lovely feeling in Iris's mind, like the fragrance of their cinnamon incense. Some of their calm strength had entered her heart. Yet she still couldn't catch the detail that was evading her in the story. Nothing stuck out as a clue.

When she got home, Helen was waiting for her with a bowl of nutritional yeast. She looked tired and sad, and Iris felt guilty that she hadn't been spending more time with her the past few days. But it would all be okay once Ares won their case.

"Iris, that science teacher of yours called."

"Really?"

"She said she had something important to talk to you about."

"Hmm, that's weird. She's really crazy." Iris ate a little yeast, just to make her mother happy.

Helen sighed, then said, "Yeah, I think the whole world's gone crazy." She took off her glasses and rubbed her eyes. "I need to tell you something, Iris. I should have told you at breakfast this morning, but I've been avoiding it . . . I lost my job at the factory, Iris. That same day I gave my big presentation. I lost it and I've been driving around, going to every lab I can think of, but no one wants a soybeantologist. I can't find a new job, and I don't know what we're going to do." Her mother started to cry, and then so did Iris.

"Mom, I'm sorry. I did something awful. I read your mail and I knew you got fired. I only did it because it was sitting . . . well, it was really bad of me to do it, and I'm sorry."

Helen shook her head. "It doesn't matter. You would have found out sooner or later. But things are serious, Iris. We're going to get evicted soon if I don't find something else to do."

Iris said eagerly, "Wait, Mom, look what I got for you! From selling your records." She reached into her pocket and gave her mother the whole $130, from Apollo and from Atlas. "Plus, it's going to be okay, Mom. I have a friend who's a really good lawyer and he's going to help us. We can sue them for firing you."

"We can't sue them, Iris. We could never afford it."

"But he said he'd only charge us if we win, and he thinks we can win a lot of money."

"Listen, Iris, they fired me for a robot. That's perfectly legal. The world changes and some people are out of luck. That's just the way it works. People get left behind."

Iris had no time to argue with her mother, because the phone rang.

"It's for you, Iris. It's that Webb woman again."

Iris picked up the receiver as if it were covered with cockroaches. The last thing she needed was to get yelled at by her crazy teacher. But Mrs. Webb surprised her.

"Iris? I hope you're feeling okay, dear?"

"Uh, yeah, I'm fine."

"Listen, sweetie. There's something very important I need to talk to you about."

Iris was worried it might be a trap of some kind. "What?"

"Listen, Iris, would you mind if I came over right now to talk?" Iris put her hand over the receiver. "She wants to come over," she whispered to her mother. Helen shook her head.

"Well, Mrs. Webb, it's been a very long day and my mother isn't feeling very well—"

"Then meet me at the Monster Burger in the strip mall. Right away. We have to talk." And Mrs. Webb hung up.

"What's that about?" Helen asked. She had wiped her tears away and was trying to eat the nutritional yeast.

"I dunno. Wants to meet me at Monster Burger to talk about something. I guess I'll go."

"It must be because you're such a good science student. All that extra research at the shore. You take after your mother."

"Yeah, I guess."

"Here, Iris." Helen counted out ten dollars. "Have a nice dinner. Get whatever you want, even if it's meat."

Chapter 26

Iris liked Monster Burger, because all the menu items were named after monsters. She was eating a Blaculaburger with Frankenfries. Mrs. Webb had ordered a Loch Ness Salad but didn't touch it. It was strange to be sitting with her teacher in a restaurant. What was even stranger was that Mrs. Webb had insisted on paying for her. Iris still had her ten dollars wadded up into a ball in one fist. She hoped nobody from her school would walk in and see her sitting with Mrs. Webb.

"So, Iris, let me get to the point. I want to apologize, first of all, for sending you to the principal today. I was out of line. In addition, I want to apologize for any time I treated you with disrespect or rudeness. I, Hillary Webb, apologize." And her teacher got up from the plastic booth and knelt down on the floor of the fast-food restaurant. She placed her forehead on Iris's sneakers. The velour alien heads of her sweat suit seemed to bow humbly.

Iris looked around the restaurant in a panic. *"Please get up, Mrs. Webb."*

"Say it! Say you forgive me, Iris!"

"I forgive you; now get up before anyone sees you!"

Mrs. Webb got up, then sat down across from Iris. "Your Celestial Highness, when I examined your blood today, I learned the error of my ways. I see now that you are what I have always been waiting for. You are a member of the alien race."

"What! Mrs. Webb, I've gotta go home." Iris got up.

"No, wait, please!" Mrs. Webb said. "Oh beautiful child of the stars, honor me with a few more minutes of your gracious time."

Iris rolled her eyes. "What do you want? Why do you think I'm an alien?"

"Your blood cells. They have a mark on them, invisible to most, but not to one who knows what to look for. And I know what to look for, since I have spent my whole life searching for evidence of our friends from the stars. So, I looked in your health files and saw that your parents are divorced and they were married only briefly—"

"Hey! You can't—"

"And I put two and two together and realized that your mother must have been forced into a hasty marriage because she was *impregnated by an alien. Iris, your father must have been a high-ranking alien commander!* Your blood cells were signed with a thunderbolt! It's the symbol of heavenly power—"

But Iris was no longer listening. Her blood cells were signed with a thunderbolt. She felt her heart pound, and she heard a roaring in her ears as she realized the detail she had missed in the story of Arachne. Iris imagined Athena looking at the magnificent tapestry of her rival. All over Arachne's work the misdeeds of the gods glittered. But there were three things that had puzzled Athena, and they were the three predictions. In the center was Athena with the bloody shuttle, predicting her violence. Around the border was the first-ever spider, predicting Arachne's fate. And there, mixed in with the scenes of Zeus's dalliances, was a woman that Athena had never seen before. *Arachne's third and last prediction was about Iris Greenwold's birth.*

Iris imagined the scene as Arachne had woven it: a young scientist, walking home from her lab in suburban Pennsylvania, quite pretty beneath her thick glasses. Zeus gazed at her from a cloud, with a lightning bolt ready in his hand and a tiny golden arrow piercing his heart. Eros hid behind an oak tree, giggling.

And Iris could figure out the rest. Her mother had gotten pregnant and either didn't understand or couldn't accept the truth: that it had been Zeus's child. Her mother, the scientist. How could she make sense of such a magical and unscientific event! So she went to synagogue for the first time in her life, and married the first man she met.

Iris came back to reality.

Mrs. Webb was on her knees again, her hands raised in prayer.

"Please, take me to your leader, Iris! I'm ready! I've been preparing for this all my life!"

Iris shook her head to clear it. Excitement pulsed through her veins. She was the daughter of Zeus! Athena and Apollo and Artemis, all of them were her brothers and sisters! Now it made perfect sense why Iris had always felt different and special and why it had been so hard to believe that the man in Wisconsin was her father.

"Iris?" Mrs. Webb was gazing up at her in supplication.

"Listen, Mrs. Webb."

"Yes?"

"I, uh, talked to my father about you already."

"Oh, really! Oh, how wonderful!"

"And he really appreciates your interest in our super-galactic culture . . . but see, we aliens just want to keep a low profile for the time being, you know? Not show ourselves to man."

"Oh, yes." Her face grew rapt. "Yes, I can understand that."

"So, it would be best if you kept our identity a secret for now, maybe even got some sweat suits with different designs. If we want to start an embassy, you're the first one we'll call."

"Oh, Iris, oh, thank you!" Mrs. Webb hugged her, which was alarming, then curtsied, which was even worse. She ran out of the restaurant in a trance of joy.

Iris sat in the booth, unable to finish her Frankenfries.

One word was going through her mind: *Zeus, Zeus, Zeus.* She got up, walked out into the twilight, and wandered beside the road. She had a magnificent, magical father. She wanted to meet him that moment. She felt that her life would be complete as soon as she met him. But she had no idea where he lived. She stomped her foot in frustration. She had forgotten to ask Athena for Zeus's address.

A horn beeped and a boy on a skateboard skidded to a stop next to her. He had a shaved head and earrings, and he wore a baggy WrestleMania T-shirt and long shorts. There was a radio implanted in his skateboard, blaring hip-hop music into the night air. Iris looked into his bright blue eyes, enchanted. He was very cute, and she couldn't be sure, but she thought she'd seen him somewhere before.

"Delivery for Iris Greenwold, from Athena." He pulled a clipboard and a small envelope out of his messenger bag and handed them to her. "Sign here, please." He pointed to a line on the clipboard, just underneath signatures of Poseidon and Apollo. Then he stamped her envelope with a rubber stamp that hung from his neck. The mark was a turtle. He cocked his head at her. "Your hair looks nice. You been seeing Aphrodite?"

Iris nodded. "Are you the same one who brought me all those packages—"

But it was too late. With a wink, the boy pushed off and was speeding away from her, going faster than any mortal skater can. Before he disappeared into the night, Iris saw the fluttering wings attached to his sneakers.

"Hermes," she whispered. Hermes liked her hair.

Chapter 27

Inside the envelope was an address in Kensington. Athena seemed to know everything! It had to be Zeus's address. Underneath it, Athena had written: "Every heroine should understand where she comes from. This helps her decide where she is going."

Iris told the rainbow to take her to the address, and in a moment found herself on a dreary block of row homes. Her father's was the one with peeling aluminum siding and a collection of wooden cows out front. The cows had lots of different themes, like the Philadelphia Eagles and "Proud to be Irish."

Iris stood on the stoop for a moment, gazing at her father's door. It had five locks on it and a tiny opening at the bottom for a cat. She could hear TV coming from somewhere in the house. She couldn't believe she would finally meet him, the king of the gods and her own, real father. Finally all her questions about herself would be answered. She knocked with a trembling hand.

A middle-aged woman answered. Her hair was up in curlers and she wore a grimy bathrobe. "Who's that, this time of night?" She scowled out at Iris and sucked on a cigarette. "If you're a Jehovah's Witness, I'm not interested. The only god I believe in is my husband. And if you're selling something, I've got no money till the first."

Iris hadn't planned what she would say. "Hello, ma'am. It's nice to meet you. My name is Iris Greenwold."

"Good for you."

"Are you Hera?"

"Yeah." She blew smoke in Iris's face.

"I, uh, I was actually hoping I could speak to your husband."

Hera's eyes narrowed. "What for?"

Iris was silent for a moment, picking her words. But Hera caught the hesitation. She switched on the stoop light and looked at Iris.

"Oh," Hera said. "I see." She dropped her cigarette and ground it out under one slipper. Then she stepped outside and closed the door behind her. With the strength of a large man, Hera lifted Iris up off the ground by her shirt. "Now you listen to me." Hera's breath reeked of cigarettes. "If you think he's gonna be happy to see you, you're wrong. My husband's had brats all through the ages, all over the globe. Whenever I turn my head, he's off messing around with some mortal woman." She dropped Iris, who fell backward down the steps. Hera leaned over her and laughed.

"You come here like you're someone special. Why didn't he ever contact you, then, if you're so special? Why didn't he ever send you money? 'Cause I can see from how you're dressed that he never sent nothing."

Iris stared wide-eyed at Hera.

"Nothin' to say, huh? Good. 'Cause we got nothin' to say to you." And Hera went back inside and slammed the door.

Iris looked at the closed door, then down at her hands. She had skinned her palms when she fell, and they beaded up with blood. Somehow, Iris couldn't cry. What Hera had said hurt too much for that. It just made Iris feel cold inside. But she'd come all this way, met all those gods . . . and then Iris understood why Athena hadn't told her right away who her father was. It wasn't just that she'd wanted Iris to have the satisfaction of discovery. It was also that all her adventures had toughened her up. She had learned from the gods and their stories. And she wasn't leaving without seeing her father. Iris reached into her backpack for the second box of beauty she'd gotten from Aphrodite. She walked back up the stairs, knelt down, and slid it through the cat door.

She waited.

And waited.

Would Hera pick it up?

It was cold, so Iris wrapped the rainbow tightly around her. She listened to the symphony of car alarms on the street, to the loud music, to the people fighting. Kensington is a rough neighborhood, and for the first time, Iris felt that maybe Middleville wasn't that bad. At least it had trees and white-tailed deer. She watched the wooden cows in their concrete pasture.

The door swung open. Hera now wore a purple sequined gown that molded itself to every inch of her figure. Her arms were white and shapely. Her eyes shone.

"You have five minutes," she said.

Iris stepped across the threshold, wrinkling her nose at the strange, other-people's-house smell. Hera had filled every inch of her home with commemorative plates, dolls, stuffed animals, and a large collection of peacock feathers. Being around all this stuff made Iris feel edgy, as if it might fall off the shelves and smother her.

"He's in the den, watching TV," Hera said. "As usual."

Iris followed the sound of the television. When she entered the den, her father's back was to her. And so the first thing she noticed was how heavy he was. His flesh spilled out of his sweatpants and over the sides of the easy chair.

Iris coughed politely.

Without turning around, he shot out, "Where's that beer I asked for?"

He thought she was Hera. "Um, I'd be happy to get you one if you tell me where they are."

Zeus spun around in his chair and fixed Iris with huge, fierce eyes. Under the pressure of that gaze, all the hair on Iris's body stood on end.

"Hmm," he said, looking her up and down. "Yeah, I remember. That pretty little scientist. It was all Eros's fault, that one. I hope you don't think I'm gonna pay child support. Eros should pay, if anybody." Zeus turned back to the TV. "They're in the fridge."

"What?" she whispered.

"THE BEER. It's in the fridge."

Iris turned and numbly walked back down the hall. Hera was sitting in the living room, staring out the front window. When she saw Iris, she pointed to the kitchen. Iris took a beer out of the refrigerator and brought it to her father.

He popped it open and licked the lid. "What's your name, kid?"

"Iris."

"Well, *Iris,* let me teach you something. When you bring a man a beer, open it first." He aimed the remote control at the television, but the back of the remote fell off and the batteries tumbled down onto the floor. "HEEEEER-AAAAA!" His voice rocked the foundations of the house. Dogs began barking across the street.

Hera leaned against the doorframe. "What."

"The remote is busted again! How many times have I told you to be careful—"

"About as many times as I've told you to stay away from mortal wom—"

"What I do in my free time and who I hang out with is my own—"

"Not while I'm still queen of the gods it's not."

He raised a meaty hand in the air. "I'm warning you, Hera!"

"You're warning me, what? You can barely stand up you're so fat. Lay one hand on me and I call the police, Ares, *and* Hephaestus. And, by the way, *look at me,* will you? I look the best I've looked in hundreds of years! And do you notice? Not a thing. You only have eyes for that TV." She stormed out.

"She did look pretty good," Zeus said. He tried to pick up the batteries at his feet but his stomach got in the way.

"Here." Iris picked the batteries up and handed them to him. She took the duct tape out of her backpack. "Why don't you duct-tape it closed so they won't fall out?"

He took the tape from her and examined it. "This is from my son."

"Yeah. He gave it to me for you."

Zeus grunted and tore off a piece with his teeth. He carefully patched up the remote control. "Thanks, kid." He pointed the remote at the TV and flipped to a channel that had women's beach volleyball. He chuckled and pointed to the TV. "*This* is the best thing about the future. Don't even have to leave your house anymore to see pretty girls. Watch the whole world go by, without lifting a finger."

"Yeah, I guess," Iris said. They sat and watched the volleyball. Her father sipped his beer. Iris felt sick to her stomach. She was grateful that Apollo had taught her the word *anticlimax,* because when you are suffering from something, it helps to know the name of the condition. Her father was nothing at all like she'd imagined. She thought back to what Athena had told her. *Truth burns.*

"Dad? Can you still throw lightning bolts?"

"Bah, what's the point of all that? I power the house now. It takes a lotta juice to keep the satellite going at the same time as the microwave."

"FIVE MINUTES!" Hera screeched from the living room.

"Ah, guess that's your cue," Zeus said. "Well, go on, ask me for something."

"What?"

"Ask me for a boon. That's why you came."

"No, I didn't. I just came to meet you."

He snorted. "Well, you met me. Bit of a disappointment, aren't I."

Iris was silent.

"Yeah, I know I am," he said. "I'm faded, like an old boxer." He threw his head back and downed the beer, then threw it onto a shoulder-high pile of cans in the corner of the room. "Sorry, you know, that I never came looking for you, or anything. I don't really like children."

"Oh."

"But I know you're mine; you've got the look. Bet you even get little electric shocks sometimes, when you touch stuff? And your hair gets more static than most people." She nodded. "Don't worry, that'll go away as you get older. Ask me for a boon, anyway. That's what's supposed to happen. River Styx." He turned the TV off and looked up at her with his wide eyes, and she imagined the way he must have been, a long, long time ago, when he was king of the world.

But Iris couldn't think of anything she wanted. All she had ever wanted her whole life was to feel special, and to have wonderful adventures. Both of those things had already happened. There *was* something Zeus could help her with, though. He seemed to have a lot of influence with Hades. If governors could get people released from death row, maybe Zeus could get Iris out of middle school.

"Do you know how you made that special deal for Persephone, where she only had to stay in hell half the time, since she'd eaten so little?"

"Mmm-hmm."

"Well, I hardly ever eat anything at the school cafeteria . . ."

"Done," he grunted.

And Iris left. But as she passed Hera, the goddess stopped her.

"Not so fast, you stealing little brat."

"What are you talking about? I didn't take anything."

"The rainbow."

Iris clutched it around her, tight. "It's mine! It was a gift from Athena. She wove it for me."

"She plagiarized. The real shawl belonged to the real Iris. And Iris was *my* servant, so all her things passed to me when she died."

"But it's *not* the real shawl. You just said that. It's a copy."

"But I own the rights to the original," said Hera. She grabbed the shawl from Iris and settled it over her own broad shoulders. "Athena was overstepping her bounds. You had your fun, and now it's back where it belongs."

"That's mean of you," Iris said. "You know I love it, and that's why you want it. I did *good things* with the rainbow. I saved Poseidon, and I went lots of places and met people and had adventures. You won't have any adventures with it. You'll never even *use* it, you'll just let it sit on a shelf and it'll get covered with dust. And they'll never hear their names again, the colors. They'll never—"

Iris cried at the thought of the rainbow folded away on a shelf in that terrible house, smelling like mothballs and cigarettes. The rainbow had made her feel like a heroine. Without it, she'd just be Iris. She drank the rainbow in with her eyes, remembering the feel of it against her skin.

"There *is* one other possibility," said Hera. She smiled a dazzling, white smile.

"What?"

There was a light in Hera's eyes. "You can have the rainbow back, and use it all you want, on one condition. You'll be my messenger, my own little messenger girl, just like in the old days." Hera took off the shawl and laid it back around Iris's shoulders. "It's easy work, being my hand-maiden. A little shopping, checking in on Zeus, that kind of thing. You'll get to be close to your father that way. You'll get to have a relationship." Hera's voice was like razor blades hidden in honey.

Iris shivered. She stroked the fabric of the shawl as she considered the bargain Hera proposed. It would be awful, having to hang around this house and having to do Hera's bidding. Iris needed to meet her father, like Athena said, so she could understand who she was. But now she knew. So perhaps the rainbow had served its purpose.

It wasn't such a hard decision, really. Without the rainbow, she would just be plain old Iris. But that wasn't such a bad thing to be. She whispered, so only the colors could hear:

"Good-bye, Πυρρός
Good-bye, Σανδαράκινος
Good-bye, Ξανθός
Good-bye, Χλωρός
Good-bye, Ὑακίνθινος
Good-bye, Πορφύρεος
Good-bye, Ἰοειδής"

And she thought she heard seven voices sing back in chorus, "Good-bye, Iris."

She handed the shawl back to Hera, who shook with rage.

"You will be sorry."

"Probably," Iris said, "but I'll get over it."

Hera slammed the door shut behind her. Iris felt bone-tired, and remembered that she hadn't slept at all the night before. It was late now, and without the rainbow, she faced a long walk home through a dangerous neighborhood. She wasn't even sure she knew the way. It was possible that she had made a foolish decision. She glanced back at Hera's door, then shook her head and set off into the night.

Iris had only walked a block when the night brightened. Up in the sky, a woman's dark face looked down at her, silhouetted against the moon. Iris's heart lifted. It was Artemis, watching over her! Then a hooting rang out through the street and an owl swooped down onto Iris's shoulder.

"Take a right at the streetlight," the bird screeched.

Two blocks later, a boy on a skateboard offered her a ride. She would not normally have gotten onto a skateboard with a stranger, but this stranger had winged sneakers and blue eyes that gave her a funny feeling in her chest. Iris held on to his waist, which was warm under her hands.

Hermes kicked off and they did a full somersault in the air, landing featherlight on the pavement. His wings flapped and his wheels sang as the little skateboard carried them through the city of Philadelphia. As they raced along, they talked of many things. Hermes told Iris about what Zeus used to be like in the old days. He told her about being a messenger and how he loved it, and how that love had kept him young through the ages. Iris told him about the rainbow and how beautiful it was. She told him about soybeans and how good they are for you. Then they were silent and watched the road.

She held on tight to Hermes, as buildings and streets and people flew by, faster and faster, until they became the buildings and the streets that Iris knew, and then the building was her own building and the street, her street. She got off the skateboard and turned to say good-bye. Hermes pulled out a guitar made from a turtle shell. He sang Iris a good-bye song. It was an old song, and had very few words: *Beautiful Lonely Road. Joy Sorrow Road.*

Iris understood just what he meant.

"Thank you, Hermes, for the ride." She headed back into the apartment building, where her mother would be waiting for her. What a ride it had been! Like all good things, it was over too soon.

Appendix

A FEW DOCUMENTS DELIVERED
BY HERMES THE FOLLOWING YEAR

DOSSIER: GREENWOLD V. TOFU-LICIOUS
FOR: ARES, J.D.
FROM: DOUBLE-A INVESTIGATION (ARTEMIS AND ATHENA)

Name of Company: Tofu-licious
Ownership: Owned by the Dweebe brothers
Other businesses owned: Rifle-licious Weapons, Tobacco-licious Cigarettes, Crude-O-licious Oil
Charitable projects supported by the Dweebe family:
- Take Back Mount Rushmore!—campaign to open Mt. Rushmore to oil drilling.
- Now You're Smokin'!—ad campaign to increase smoking among inner-city youth.
- Art Fun for Everyone!—campaign to turn art museums into shooting ranges with works of art as targets.

Espionage report: CEO Norman Dweebe (married with children) is having an affair with a seventeen-year-old robot from the human resources division. VP George Dweebe is addicted to the fumes from cherry-scented Magic Markers, which he buys in bulk from a kindergarten-supply company. VP Dick Dweebe has a double life as a flamenco dancer in Madrid, which he keeps secret from his whole family.

TOFU-LICIOUS

April 14, 2006

Dear Mr. Ares,

We at Tofu-licious are appalled by your blatant attempts to blackmail us. These kinds of tactics will have no effect on a business—and a family—as upstanding as ours. None of us has anything to hide.

Please send me the negatives of those photos at once. Warmest regards,

J. Norman Dweebe
CEO, Tofu-licious, Inc.

Jdweebe@tofulicious.com
www.tofulicious.com

A Dweebe Enterprises Company
55 Faux Food Drive • Middleville, PA 19050
tel 215-555-5555

TOFU-LICIOUS ────────────────

HUNGRY FOR A CHANGE? TRY TOFU-LICIOUS!

April 21, 2006

Dear Mr. Ares,
   All right, fine. But no more than twenty million.
Warmest regards,

J. Norman Dweebe
CEO, Tofu-licious, Inc.

Jdweebe@tofulicious.com
www.tofulicious.com

A Dweebe Enterprises Company
55 Faux Food Drive • Middleville, PA 19050
tel 215-555-5555

Merman Monthly

The world's most popular underwater magazine!

REKINDLED LOVE FOR SEA GOD, GODDESS

Wedding bells are in the air for Poseidon and Amphitrite, and they're hoping that the second time's the charm. Yes, all you single mermaids can give up hopes of reeling in the King of the Sea. He's taken, and from what we hear, he's happy about it!

Porpoise paparazzi spotted the divine couple riding chartered dolphins bound for the Greek isles. Amphitrite was radiant in sea foam and pearls, while Poseidon wore a vintage wet suit by Jacques Cousteau. The couple plans to renew their vows in front of an intimate gathering of gods and octopi. We're hoping for an invitation, since we hear Dionysus is tending bar.

Tofu Is Serious Business

PHILADELPHIA, PA

There's a mother-daughter team in suburban Pennsylvania out to change the way a nation eats. Rainbow Tofu was founded by Dr. Helen Greenwold and her thirteen-year-old daughter, Iris, on the site of the bankrupt Tofu-licious, Inc. And what started as a small, family operation has grown into a national sensation.

"They've put tofu back on the map!" raves rapper Pandora, one of Rainbow's many celebrity clients. Her favorite flavor is Gangsta Grape, but Rainbow offers 92 flavors of tofu in all, from Artichoke to Zabaglione.

Part of Rainbow's appeal to today's consumer is its socially conscious image. "We are working for a better world," says Dr. Greenwold. "Our factory is completely solar-powered and has zero environmental impact." Not only that, but 50 percent of the company's profits go toward the Poseidon Institute, which boasts the largest collection of phosphorescent octopi in the world.

It's all in the family at Rainbow, where the mother heads up the technical side of things, and the daughter—released from eighth grade for half the year to work with her mother—handles the people side of the business. "My hiring philosophy," says Iris, "is to ask myself: If I had a dozen oysters, would I want to share them with this person? If the answer is yes, we hire them."

The philosophy seems to be working, because Rainbow has one of the most diverse and loyal groups of employees anywhere. Benefits include full health and dental, an on-site adventure labyrinth, and live jazz on the factory floor.

One middle manager we interviewed, a man named Sisyphus, said, "This is the best job I've ever had. My life was hell before I came here. Iris Greenwold is a goddess, I tell you, an absolute goddess."

With people like that on her side, it's no wonder Iris's rainbow ended with a pot of gold.

Note to the Reader

When the ancient Romans conquered Greece, they gave new names to the old Greek gods.

This book uses the Greek names, but many other books use the Roman names, so it's a good idea to know both.

When in doubt, ask a goddess which she prefers:

GREEK NAME	ROMAN NAME
Aphrodite	Venus
Apollo	Apollo
Ares	Mars
Artemis	Diana
Athena	Minerva
Demeter	Ceres
Dionysus	Bacchus

GREEK NAME	ROMAN NAME
Eros	Cupid
Hades	Dis
Hephaestus	Vulcan
Hera	Juno
Hermes	Mercury
Persephone	Proserpine
Poseidon	Neptune
Zeus	Jupiter

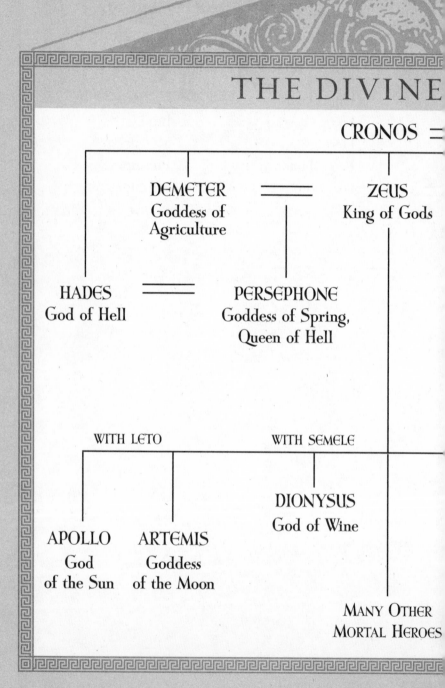

THE DIVINE

CRONOS =

DEMETER ===== ZEUS
Goddess of King of Gods
Agriculture

HADES ===== PERSEPHONE
God of Hell Goddess of Spring,
Queen of Hell

WITH LETO   WITH SEMELE

DIONYSUS
God of Wine

APOLLO   ARTEMIS
God   Goddess
of the Sun of the Moon

MANY OTHER
MORTAL HEROES

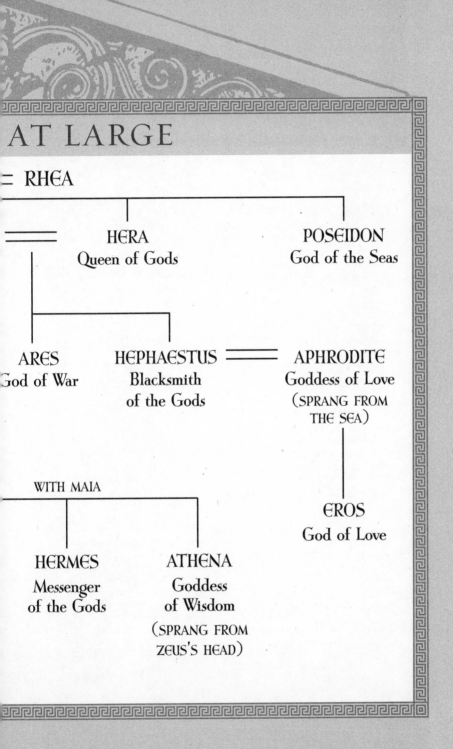

= RHEA

HERA
Queen of Gods

POSEIDON
God of the Seas

ARES
God of War

HEPHAESTUS
Blacksmith
of the Gods

APHRODITE
Goddess of Love
(SPRANG FROM
THE SEA)

WITH MAIA

EROS
God of Love

HERMES
Messenger
of the Gods

ATHENA
Goddess
of Wisdom
(SPRANG FROM
ZEUS'S HEAD)